BLEEDING HEARTS

BOOK TWO OF THE POISON GARDEN

JENNIFER ALLIS PROVOST

BELLATRIX PRESS

Bellatrix Press

First Edition

Chapter 1

Shiny, Like Medusa

I read the business's street number off the side of the building, then I checked it against the scrap of paper in my hand. "This is it?"

"According to my divination spell, yes." Tessa tossed her bouncy, shiny hair behind her shoulder, and the dark strands reflected the morning light like polished onyx. Tessa was a living, breathing shampoo commercial. "What's so unusual about it?"

"For starters, it's a Chinese restaurant, and Nathaniel Beauclaire's a witch who was born in tenth century England."

Tessa shrugged, sending all those perfectly loose waves cascading over her shoulder once again. She was like Medusa, but shiny. "Hiding out in a foreign culture's neighborhood is a common tactic that those on the run have used since time immemorial."

"I don't know if one restaurant qualifies as a neighborhood." The city we lived in didn't have a Chinatown, or any other cultural hubs to speak of. The city council liked to refer to themselves as diverse and inclusive, but once you got past the four blocks that comprised the downtown area, it was upper middle class Caucasians as far as the eye could see.

"And doesn't Nathaniel prefer expensive places?" I added. "I can't see him hanging out near an all you can eat lunch buffet."

"Hence the 'hiding out' aspect, as I said earlier." Tessa leaned closer to the window, shielding her eyes as she scoped out the darkened interior. "I don't see anyone, and the lights are off. Let's go inside."

I sighed, then I knelt in front of the door and got to work picking the lock. Tessa could have unlocked the door in a hot second with her witchcraft, but if Nathaniel really was inside, if she used her magic, it might alert him to our presence. We'd been tracking him for too long, and had experienced too many close calls, to make a rookie mistake now.

In addition to Nathaniel, we were also on the lookout for his murderous mother-in-law, Sarah Allwood. She'd died several hundred years ago, but her incredibly powerful spirit had hung around to make life miserable for her descendants. Most recently, she'd possessed a childhood friend of mine, Jada, for the past twenty years. At the time, Sarah had been attempting to possess me, all with the ultimate goal of merging her considerably strong witchcraft with my seer abilities. As much as I wish Jada had never been possessed at all, I was so, so grateful I'd dodged that bullet.

It didn't take me long to disengage the lock. It hadn't been a very challenging lock, which was the latest disappointment in our increasingly frustrating pursuit of Nathaniel. Ever since Nathaniel was revealed as Cecily Allwood's co-conspirator in the death of her brother, Jacob, Tess and I had been tracking Nathaniel, intending to stop him once and for all. For Tessa, that meant sending him off this mortal coil to finally be with his much loved and already deceased wife, Jemima. I wasn't down with such a final solution, and was hoping to incapacitate him with a binding spell instead. Tessa had agreed to consider the binding spell and other non-lethal options, but she hadn't made any promises.

I pushed open the restaurant's door. It went as easily as the lock had. "This is not a secure location," I observed.

"Is it still in business?" Tessa entered the dark restaurant and stood next to the hostess station. She ran a finger over the shiny wood menu stand. "Not a speck of dust."

"Weird." I stepped behind the bar, which was stocked for the lunch rush right down to the full ice bin. "The ice hasn't even melted. Where's the bartender, and the cooks? The waitresses?"

"And where are all the customers?" Tess added. She pulled a piece of spelled paper out of her back pocket and flung it into the air. It hung immobile for a moment, then it disintegrated into a cloud of rainbow-hued dust. "We're not under a stasis spell. So where is everyone?"

"Could Nathaniel have made everyone invisible?"

Tessa gave me a look. "It's easier to kill someone and trap their spirit than to cast a proper invisibility spell."

Before I could ask how the hell she knew that, my phone chirped. "Goddammit," I hissed.

"Turn that off," Tessa said. "You'll alert Nathaniel."

"As if he can't hear us talking. If he's even here." I withdrew my phone and glanced at the screen. It was a text from Dan.

Dan: You free?
Eli: I'm breaking into a Chinese restaurant. You?
Dan: I am going to assume that's a joke.

"Making a date?" Tessa looked over my shoulder. "Oh, tell Dan I said hello."

"You are so nosy."

Eli: Tess says hi. What's up?
Dan: Hey, Tessa.
Dan: The new track at the college is complete. Want to go for a run?

"You should go," Tessa said. "It's been months since you two had your moment. You need to rekindle that spark."

"There is no spark," I muttered. "At least, there shouldn't be."

Before I could fire off a response to Dan, I felt a familiar tingle on the back of my neck. "There's a spirit nearby," I said.

"Let's hope they're friendly," Tessa murmured.

I cleared my throat, and said, "You can come closer. We won't hurt you."

Nothing happened, and no one materialized. "You're certain one is nearby?" Tessa asked.

"Yeah." I came out from behind the bar and followed the sensation into the kitchen. "It's stronger in here." My neck warmed. "It feels... angry."

Tessa entered the kitchen and leaned against the salad station. Like everything else, the day's ingredients had been prepped and were waiting to be assembled. "Maybe it's a former owner, or someone who used to work here? A disgruntled employee could be angry." She swiped a slice of cucumber from a stainless steel bin. "Vegetables are fresh."

"Yeah. Maybe the spirit is a former cook." What was extremely strange was that I felt the spirit as plain as day, but they hadn't come forward when I spoke to them. Some ghosts hung around places for years waiting for someone to notice them. Here I was, ready to interact, and they were hiding from me. Why would they do that?

What if someone had used them to lay a trap?

"Tess, I think we should get out of here."

"Why?" she asked, and I heard something click behind me.

I turned around. The clicks had come from the stove.

My phone chirped; it was another text from Dan.

Dan: Run. Yes or No?
Eli: One sec.

As I watched, the knobs on the stove turned to the "on" position. Then the gas ignited and flames shot toward the ceiling.

"Get down," I shrieked as I dove under the worktable. I couldn't see Tessa, but I heard metal clattering like hail on a tin roof. I stuck my hand out but snatched it back when something hit me. Knives bounced off the stainless steel worktable and hit the floor around me like the world's deadliest rainfall.

And they kept falling. Dozens of knives—all of them wickedly sharp cooking blades—rained down from the ceiling, so many knives that the fallen ones piled up in the corners like snowdrifts.

"Why does this place have so much cutlery?" I yelled.

"I don't think they're real," Tessa yelled back, then the clattering stopped. I waited for a moment, then I got out from under the table. Tessa was right. The knives were gone.

"Tess," I called. "Tessa, are you okay?"

"I'm fine." I heard movement near the salad station. Tessa stood up and brushed lettuce leaves and shredded carrots off her arms. "I'm covered in vegetables, but otherwise unharmed."

"I guess Nathaniel really was here." Something on the counter caught my eye; it was an old-fashioned metal buckle, the kind young kids wore on Pilgrim hats in school plays. "Why is this here?"

"Why is what here?" Tessa asked, then stopped short when she saw the buckle. "Oh."

"Oh, what?"

"Nathaniel's surname, Beauclaire, is derived from *bouclier*. It means buckle maker."

I picked up the buckle. "I guess that makes this evidence."

My phone chirped. I picked up my phone—luckily, the screen hadn't shattered—and saw that Dan had texted again. "Are we done here?"

Tessa plucked a radish out of her hair. "Oh, we're done all right."

Eli: I could use a run. Meet you there in an hour?
Dan: Sounds like a plan.

I slid my phone into my pocket and turned to Tessa. "Getting attacked with knives is a new and awful thing."

"At least they weren't real," she replied. "Where's our ghost?"

"Gone." I looked at the stove, and the knobs that turned on the gas. With enough energy, a ghost could definitely manage turning them, but that didn't explain the knives. It made me wonder if I'd senses a ghost, or something else. "What are the chances of Nathaniel recruiting a ghost to work for him?"

Tessa gazed at the ruined kitchen. "I'd say the chances are good."

Chapter 2

It's a Nice Track

I arrived at Braerton College about ninety minutes after Tess and I left the restaurant. The college had recently gotten a grant to refurbish the outdoor athletic area, which included a new track. The ribbon cutting ceremony had happened just last week. I hadn't attended, but Dan had as a representative from the police department. I saw him on the news, not that I'd been looking for him. He had looked nice in his charcoal gray suit, though.

When I arrived at the track, I saw him stretching and took a moment to admire the view. Never in a million years would I have suspected that cops were muscular underneath their uniforms, but Detective Daniel Lyons had a body like a cover model from a trashy romance novel. Today he was wearing a blue athletic shirt, black running shorts, and black sneakers. I momentarily wished I'd worn shorts, since it was already getting hot. Running in summer isn't for the heat sensitive.

"Hey," I called. Dan stopped stretching and looked up, then he smiled and my heart nearly skipped a beat. Not only was Dan in great shape, he had curly dark hair, big brown eyes, and a smile that could turn your day around. No two ways about it, he was handsome, and smart, and fun to be around, which actually made it all the more frustrating to be around him.

Tessa had been trying to broker a date between Dan and me ever since she first met Officer Muscleman, which was what she liked to call him. I hoped he never caught on to that nickname. At first, I resisted going out with Dan because he's a mortal, whereas I'm a seer. Historically, matches between mortals and the magical community didn't work out. My parents were living proof of that. Then Dan had stumbled into a situation involving Nathaniel Beauclaire—Dan claims he was rescuing me, but he'd gotten tied up in the basement just like I had—where I ended up exorcising Sarah Allwood's spirit from my old friend, Jada. Ever since he landed headfirst in the supernatural world, I'd agreed to always be straight with him, no matter what. He'd turned out to be a great partner, and an even better friend.

Then there was that time we'd kissed, and it had been amazing. Dan had made it clear that he was attracted to me, and I'd be lying if I said I didn't feel anything in return. In the months since we shared that single, perfect kiss, we'd worked on many more cases and become true friends, and I wanted to keep it that way. I'd had precious few good friends in my life, and I didn't want to risk what I'd built with Dan over something that might not amount to more than a summer fling. The path I'd chosen was definitely the more boring option, but I was confident it was the right thing to do.

I still thought about that kiss.

"I thought you stood me up," Dan called back.

"Sorry," I said. "I had to drop off Tessa, and change."

Dan looked over my outfit. I was wearing a black tank top, my usual running shoes, and my brand new purple running tights, which I may or may not have been saving for my next run with Dan. "Well, you look great."

My cheeks warmed, but I could blame that on the hot day. Speaking of which... "It's supposed to get up over eighty degrees by noon," I said. "Should we really be running in this heat?"

"Come on, we gotta try out the new track," he said. "One lap, then I'll buy you an iced coffee."

"You do know the way to my heart."

"Do I?" he asked, grinning. Before I could say anything I might regret, I took off running, leaving Dan to catch up. He was right, it was a nice track.

After we finished our lap—I'd won, as usual—we walked across campus to the coffee kiosk. Thanks to the year round class schedule, it was always open. Dan bought us two iced coffees, and we found a table in the shade.

"Were you really breaking into a restaurant earlier?" he asked.

"Maybe." I took a long drink of coffee. They made it with whole milk and no sugar, just the way I liked it. "Tessa had a lead on Beauclaire."

"And?"

"And what? He wasn't there, just like he's never where we think he is."

"I'd say he's a ghost, but if he was, you'd probably have a handle on things."

I glared at him. "Ha ha." Dan grinned. I rolled my eyes and leaned back, looking around the campus. A group of bright pink flowers near the coffee kiosk caught my eye.

"Weird."

"What's weird?"

"That plant." I took a picture of it with my phone, then used a plant identification app to confirm what I already knew. "It's called bleeding hearts."

"Let me guess, it's poisonous?"

"Don't worry. I won't let the mean flower hurt you." Dan didn't rise to the bait. In addition to being intelligent and good looking, he was patient. "What's interesting is that they go dormant in summer, yet here we are in the first week of August and it's in full bloom."

"Think it has anything to do with Beauclaire? Like the apple orchard blooming out of season?" he asked.

"It could be related." I set down my phone and said, "Earlier, at the restaurant, we found an old, out-of-place buckle. Tessa thinks it has something to do with Nathaniel."

"Interesting. Where can we learn more about this magic buckle?"

"We could ask Bennet," I said. "He should be in his office now. It's right across campus."

Dan stood and offered me a hand. "I've got time if you do."

I let him help me up, then I dropped his hand so I could fix my ponytail. "We can check out the progress on the new greenhouse while we're there."

"Based on what happened to the last greenhouse, maybe the school should steer clear of one for a while." The burned-out hulk of the old greenhouse remained in place, scorch marks from the lightning strikes and all. Apparently, the grant the school used to refurbish the athletic department didn't extend to horticultural cleanup.

"Don't say that to Bennet. You'll break his leafy heart."

We crossed the central green and headed toward the science division. Bennet Carrington was Braerton's head horticulturist, but I knew him because he was an old friend of Gran's. Bennet was a shepherd, but not the kind who tended livestock. In the seer community, shepherds kept track of knowledge, like family histories, land ownership, and grimoires. It seemed like an old-fashioned and somewhat outdated occupation, but most people in the supernatural community were very old—Tessa remembered when tobacco was first introduced to Europe—and weren't interested in learning about modern things like the internet.

Next to the science building was a fenced off area, with a sign that proclaimed it as the future site of the horticulture department's new greenhouse.

"Odd they haven't broken ground yet," Dan said. "You'd think they'd want this taken care of before fall classes start up."

"Do you break ground for a greenhouse?" I wondered as we stepped inside the building. "Maybe they'll just set it on top of the grass."

"That wouldn't be very secure."

"What, you're a foreman now?"

"Might as well be. I do plenty of work around my own house."

I stumbled. Dan shot out a hand to steady me. "You all right?"

"Yeah. Thanks."

I flashed him a quick smile, then I started up the stairs toward Bennet's office. I'd never once been to Dan's house, even though he was at my apartment-slash-office at least twice a week, and I was a regular visiting him at the police station. Because the internet is a thing I knew where Dan lived, and that it was a single family home in a nice neighborhood, but that was the extent of my snooping.

I glanced at Dan over my shoulder. He was hovering behind me like I might fall at any moment. "Do you do a lot of work on your house?"

"The joys of home ownership." I'd noticed that he was reticent to talk about his place, which was odd. Dan was an open book, and hadn't shied away from anything I'd ever asked him, no matter how gross or awkward. I wondered if he was holding back because I was, and decided to test that theory.

"I bet. Gran's house always needs something, like shingles or plumbing or yard work. It's exhausting."

"I could help you. If you wanted help, that is."

"Thanks. I might take you up on that."

We reached the third floor, which was where the tenured professors had their offices. Bennet's space wasn't technically an office, but a repurposed sitting area at the far end of the corridor. It had a wall of south-facing windows, and he'd insisted he needed that space for the excellent sun exposure. Based on how the college went along with Bennet's many whims, sometimes I wondered if he was using some of his hoarded magical knowledge to cast compliance spells on the administrators.

"Bennet?" I called. "Are you in?"

"I am," he announced as he stepped out from behind a massive bookshelf. Shepherds weren't immortal, but they didn't age like regular humans. Bennet had appeared to be in his late forties or early fifties since I was in grade school, and he dressed like a dapper gentlemen from post-World War II London. Gran had thought that shepherds absorbed a measure of the magic they were constantly exposed to, and it kept them youthful. I didn't know if that was the case, but all shepherd's carefully guarded their past lives and never disclosed their ages. It made one wonder what they were hiding.

"Good to see you, Eli, Detective," Bennet continued as he and Dan shook hands. "Are you here to discuss the ceremony?"

"Um, no." A few months ago, I'd decided to take on my grandmother's former role as Mistress of Seers. I'd avoided being in positions of authority my entire life, and the last thing I wanted was to become the person with the most sway in the supernatural community. But when things came to a head with Cecily Allwood, I realized how easily things could get out of hand without someone overseeing things. That and, aside from my father, Gran didn't have any other living descendants.

Based on that lack of descendants, no one needed a ceremony to declare me the new Mistress, but Bennet was a stickler for traditions.

"Is there a title other than Mistress?" I asked, hoping to distract Bennet from his party planning. "I don't feel like the mistress of anything."

"Yes, well, I imagine you wouldn't." Bennet took off his glasses and polished the lenses with his handkerchief. "I suppose you can call yourself whatever you'd like. Tell me, what brings the two of you to by today?"

"We were trying out the new track," I replied. "I saw the sign for the new greenhouse."

Bennet frowned. "That's a bit of a sore subject. The board isn't sure the new structure should be so close to the academic buildings, in light of what happened to the last greenhouse."

"They can't possibly be holding a lightning strike against you," Dan said.

"In academia, grudges far outweigh good judgement," Bennet replied. "I've reams of paperwork dealing with such nonsense."

"Speaking of nonsense, Tessa and I found this earlier." I produced the buckle. "We're wondering if it might somehow be connected to Nathaniel Beauclaire."

Bennet accepted the buckle, setting his glasses aside as he scrutinized the object. "I suppose it could be. I don't recognize it, but an object this rough certainly isn't what one would expect of something connected to the Beauclaires, or the Allwoods."

"It was just a theory of Tessa's. If you have time, could you research it?"

"I always have time for you, Eli." Bennet put the buckle on his desk and grabbed a folder. "I've also got some news for you about Jada. She's going to be released from the inpatient ward at the hospital, and placed in a halfway house."

"She is? Is that good?" I asked.

"Which halfway house?" Dan asked. "Some are pretty rough. Is that the best place for her?"

"She can't remain in hospital indefinitely," Bennet said. "They've treated her as much as they can. Jada will now need to come to terms with what's happened to her, and attempt to reenter society."

"As if it's that easy." Bennet handed me the folder and I flipped through it. It contained Jada's most recent psychiatric evaluation, copies of recent physical examinations and bloodwork, and her discharge paperwork. "How did you get this?"

"I have my ways," Bennet replied. "What's most troubling is that Jada is at the mercy of her doctors. She has no family to intervene on her behalf."

"Think Beauclaire isolated her on purpose?" Dan asked.

"That is a strong possibility," Bennet replied. "Either by happenstance or by design, Jada is alone in the world."

I snapped the folder shut, then I handed it to Dan. "What should we do? According to her evaluation she's a mentally competent adult. It's not like we can adopt her."

"Eli, you were her friend," Bennet said. "Have you had any luck on that front?"

"Not really." I'd visited Jada in the hospital a few times, but it was difficult connecting with someone who still thought and acted like a nine year old. "We don't have much in common."

"Maybe you don't need to have much in common," Dan said. "Maybe Jada just needs to know that someone's on her side."

"Yeah. Maybe." Jada and I had been inseparable in grade school. If she hadn't been possessed, and my mother hadn't sent me to a psych ward of my own, we might still be friends today. "Bennet, I hate to ask you for another favor."

He adjusted his glasses and smiled. "Ask away, please."

"Can you see what other records you can get from the hospital? Jada must have family somewhere, and they might have visited her. Dan, can you look into the halfway house she's going to?"

"Sure can." Dan snapped a picture of the halfway house's information with his phone, then he handed the folder back to Bennet. "If this is one of the trashy places, I'll find out what it takes to get her transferred."

"Thanks, guys. I know Jada would thank you, too, if she knew."

We let Bennet get back to work. As Dan and I jogged down the stairs, he asked, "What will you do next?"

"Exactly what you suggested." I pushed open the double doors and squinted at the bright sun. The weather report was right, it was hot. "I'm going to look in on Jada and figure out what she needs."

"You're taking my advice? Has hell finally frozen over?"

"Not in this heat."

"I take it another lap's out of the question, then."

I wanted to say yes. "We have work to do," I said. "Besides, I need a shower."

Dan pursed his lips. "There are so many things I could say right now, but I am a gentleman. I'm gonna run a bit longer, then get started on the halfway house. I'll call you when I know something."

"Sounds good."

I watched Dan jog toward the track, half of me wanting to join him. There wouldn't be any harm in spending a few more hours with him; I'd already started a file on Jada back at the office, and after Tessa had revealed that the man masquerading as Jada's brother was actually Nathaniel Beauclaire I'd researched her immediate family. As it turned out Jada's actual surname was Morales, and she had been an only child, just like me. Maybe that's what we could bond over.

Just as I made up my mind to spend a bit more time with Dan—as friends, nothing more—I spied another patch of hot pink next to the walkway. It was a second bleeding heart, also in full bloom in the middle of summer. I picked a stalk of flowers, and started walking toward my car. Now I had a second mystery to solve.

Chapter 3

Killer Brownies

When I got back to my apartment, I found a glass, put the bleeding hearts in it with some water, and brought the whole thing into my office. I set the glass next to my computer and stared at the little pink flowers, all dangling in a pretty little row from their arched stalk. I'd never heard a single story about bleeding hearts blooming in midsummer, yet here they were in all their glory. Then again, I'd also never heard of apples being ready to harvest in April, but that had happened a few short months ago.

Maybe these flowers are enchanted. I pressed the tattoo on my left wrist against one of the flowers. The tattoo was my seer's mark, and in addition to proclaiming me an intermediary between the living and the dead, it acted like a magical bloodhound with regard to spelled items. If these flowers had been enchanted, my tattoo would recognize it and alert me.

I felt nothing.

Not to be deterred, I fished out my witchfinder—an amulet Tessa had made for me years ago—and dangled it in front of the stalk. In the presence of witchcraft, the amulet heated up. When I touched the amulet, it was stone cold.

Huh. Evidently this plant had not been touched by magic, yet it was blooming months later than it should be. Just when I was about to chalk it up to a random fluke, I remembered the bleeding hearts near the coffee stand that had also been in full bloom. That, and the fact that random fluke's never happened in my life. Instead, every detail was connected to the over-arching mystery of why the universe loved tormenting me.

Gran would tell me to stop being so dramatic. I opened my laptop, intending to research what natural events could make these unseasonable flowers happen, when the office phone rang.

"Nine Lives Investigations."

"It's me," Tessa said.

"Why are you calling the office line?"

"I was going to leave a message. I was also hoping you'd still be with Dan, but that dream's dying on the vine, now isn't it?"

"Why do you want me to date him so badly?"

"It doesn't have to be Dan, but I wish you would date someone. I worry about you being all alone."

"I'm not alone," I said, but Tessa was right. Other than her and Gran's cats—who weren't even living cats—I didn't have anyone I regularly spent time with. I talked to my dad all the time, but that was either by phone or email, since he was always traveling. I interacted with Bennet, too, but seers and shepherds had a strange hierarchy that I didn't agree with, and Bennet followed to a tee. Now that I was set to formally take on Gran's role as Mistress of Seers—assuming we couldn't figure out a better title—Bennet definitely saw me as his superior.

That left only one other person I saw on a regular basis. Dan. "I don't think I'm ready for anything like what you're thinking," I said.

"But when will you be?" Tessa said. "Eli, it's been years since you broke things off with Amir."

"Yeah, well." Amir had been my first real boyfriend. He'd been the center of my world, and I'd been willing to leave my life and family behind and follow him to the ends of the earth. He'd felt the same, but only because he wanted to be a part of the Moore legacy. Once Amir found out that there was no family dynasty for him to scam his way into, or pile of riches in the basement, he'd moved on.

I wouldn't say I'd been devastated when Amir left me. I will say that Tessa and I ate an inordinate and unhealthy amount of chocolate. It was also when we took up baking, and our killer brownie recipe was the best thing to come out of that debacle. I hadn't had a serious relationship since then, unless you counted said brownies.

"Anyway," I said; reliving my past relationships was not how I wanted to spend my afternoon. "What were you going to leave a message about?"

"I went back to the restaurant, and it was packed. Workers, customers, everything."

"But it was completely empty when we were there!"

"I asked the bartender if they'd closed down earlier today. She claimed that the restaurant had opened at nine, as it has done every day for the last sixteen years." Tessa paused, and added, "She could really use a vacation."

"We were there after nine." I grabbed my phone and checked my camera roll. I'd taken a picture of the restaurant's sign when we arrived, and the timestamp was nine thirty-eight. "Even though we were there well after when she said they opened, the place was deserted."

"Yes, it was. Therefore, the question becomes, where were the people? Or, where were we?"

"We?" I repeated. "You don't think we actually moved to a different plane, do you?"

"Maybe not a different dimension, but perhaps a different time," Tessa replied. "If Nathaniel has a time spell up his sleeve, it would explain why we always find him, but arrive at his location a moment too late."

"It sure would." I poked at the dangling flowers. "What do you know about bleeding hearts?"

"As in, overly sympathetic people?"

"No, as in the flower. I found some in full bloom."

"Odd. As far as I know, they're not used in many spells, other than love spells."

I waited for her to make a comment about me hooking up with Dan. When it didn't come, I said, "Hmm, maybe they're blooming now because of a spell gone wrong."

"That's probably it. I'm going to pick up a few things, then head home. Unless you need me for anything?"

"I'm good, thanks. I think I'll visit Jada."

"Good luck with that."

"Thanks."

We ended the call, and I sat there staring at the flowers. While I didn't doubt Tessa, I didn't think the bleeding hearts were the result of a rogue love spell. For one thing, who would cast a love spell at the college's coffee stand? Even I didn't love coffee that much. Besides, if that was the case, either my tattoo or the witchfinder would have picked up on the residual magic. No, these flowers were blooming now for an entirely different reason, and while I was curious, they would have to be put on the back burner for now. I had more important things to deal with, like figuring out what to do about Jada.

After a quick shower and snack, I was ready to visit Jada at the hospital. I didn't need to keep checking in on her, but I also couldn't forget that the only reason she'd been possessed by Sarah Allwood was because Sarah's spirit had been aiming for me, and landed in Jada instead. That happened when we were eight years old, and Jada had lost twenty years of her life while that crazy dead woman drove her body around like a sports car.

The crux of the plot was that Sarah had wanted to take full advantage of my seer abilities so she could exert influence over the living and the dead. Once that was accomplished, they would find a suitable host for the spirit of Sarah's daughter, Jemima, who was Nathaniel's deceased wife. Sarah had been holding her spirit captive for over a hundred years, and while I could understand Nathaniel's desperation, he was just as despicable as Sarah.

When the original plan had gone awry, Sarah and Nathaniel doubled down on their sadism. Sarah stayed in Jada's body, and Nathaniel had me kidnapped when I was seventeen to become a host for Jemima. I escaped before that happened, thanks to my father and Tessa, but we didn't know Jada had been possessed until a few months ago when Nathaniel returned to the area. I'd exorcised Sarah from Jada, and now her doctors claimed she was ready to go out into the world. I hoped they were right about that.

I arrived at Jada's private room on the fifth floor and knocked. Between my family's resources and Bennet's way with forms, we'd gotten Jada the best care money could buy while also remaining anonymous. I didn't want to become known as a benefactor to people with bizarre medical conditions. What with spirits, ghost hunters, and witches regularly turning up on my doorstep, I had enough on my plate.

"Come in."

I entered Jada's room and found her reading a magazine next to the window. I'd been bringing her lots of reading material, hoping she would get caught up on current affairs. So far she was only interested in the magazines that catered to middle school girls, but I caught her reading Jane Austen a few weeks ago. Mr. Darcy hasn't lost his charm.

"Hey, Eli," she said with a grin. "Did you hear I'm getting out?"

"I did," I replied. "How do you feel about that?"

"Good, I guess." She drew her knees up to her chest and wrapped her arms around her legs. "Kinda scared."

"I bet. Did they tell you where you'll be going?"

"Not yet. There's been some discussion." She glanced toward the door. Once she was certain no one was standing close enough to hear her, she leaned closer, and said, "The doctors want me in one place that has tons of services, but my case worker wants me to be more independent."

"And what do you want?"

Jada shrugged. "I just want to understand why I can't remember anything."

My heart clenched. "I wish I knew where you'd been all these years. If I did, I'd tell you all about it."

"We really didn't hang out after the third grade?"

"We really did not," I replied. I'd told her all about how my mother had put me in a psych ward and then removed herself from my life, and how I'd gone on to live with Gran. "After I went to live with my grandmother, I ended up in a different school."

"I guess both of our lives were turned upside down." She worried the edge of the table. "I think I had a boyfriend while I was... wherever I was."

"Really?" I asked, doing my best to sound calm while I was screaming inside. "What was his name?"

"Nathaniel."

I took a breath. "Has he come to see you?"

"No," she said, rather petulantly until I remembered she was mentally a nine-year-old. "No one comes to see me except you. Not even my parents."

"Do they know you're here?" We'd located Jada's parents, but since she was an adult—and the Moore trust was paying for her care—they hadn't needed to be involved.

"Yeah. They called. I think they're mad at me."

"Did they say why?"

"No, but that's how they are. Dad gets angry and Mom gets quiet, and I sit there and wonder what I did wrong." Jada's brow tensed, then she added, "Well, that's what I used to do. I don't know what happens now."

"If you want, after you're discharged I can take you to see them," I offered. "Maybe everything will be different in person."

"Yeah, I guess. Want to watch a movie?"

"Sure."

Jada turned on the television and flipped through the channels, while my thoughts careened around my head. Jada had never before mentioned any sort of memory from when she was possessed, but today she said Nathaniel's name. She referred to him as her boyfriend. That was both terrifying and odd, because even though Nathaniel had been masquerading as Jada's brother, Nick, she'd had no memory of him before today. She hadn't even recognized his picture. If her memories were returning, who knows what she might reveal.

CHAPTER 4

MEMORIES, YOUR OWN OR SOMEONE ELSE'S

INSTEAD OF A MOVIE, Jada and I watched three episodes of a comedy series she liked, during which she laughed like a hyena, and I hardly noticed the jokes. She didn't make any further references to Nathaniel, but the fact that she thought he was her boyfriend was enough. What the hell had Nathaniel been doing to her for all those years?

And let's not forget, Nathaniel's mother-in-law had possessed Jada. Eew.

Aside from the stomach-turning horror about the possible nature of Nathaniel and Jada's relationship, if Jada's memories were returning, she might hold the key to stopping Nathaniel Beauclaire and Sarah Allwood once and for all. Neither I nor Tessa had heard any mention of Sarah over the past few months, but it was well established that she was as powerful as a spirit as she had been as a living witch, maybe more so. Counting her out would be a mistake.

I needed to talk to someone about this most recent development and plan my next move. After I left the hospital, I reached for my phone to call Dan, and hesitated. I'd just seen him that morning, and he said he would call me when he had some information on the halfway house Jada was being transferred to. I could wait to talk to him. Besides, I didn't want to become dependent on him to help me solve all my problems. Instead, I drove to the eastern side of town, and to the Allwood Compound.

Jacob Allwood had been in charge of his clan's operations for the better part of a century. His sister, Cecily, murdered him to gain control of the family, but just like his ancestor, Sarah, Jacob was an unusually strong and resilient ghost. When things reached a crisis point with Cecily, I'd ended up feeding undead energy to Jacob, which made him even more powerful. His spirit had ended up gaining a solidity that I'd never encountered before, except for Gran's cats. According to Bennet, such lifelike spirits were possible, but rare. In fact, Jacob's spirit was so solid and lifelike that he'd resumed managing the family empire, and almost no one knew he was actually a ghost.

Well, that wasn't exactly true. It had been a minor scandal when Jacob was found dead—poisoned by oleander, no less—sitting at the kitchen table in a house he didn't live in. The Allwoods had enough money and influence to squash the media and seal the autopsy and coroner reports, but they couldn't do much about what people remembered reading, or about those who'd seen his body with their own eyes. Whenever someone brought up that Jacob had been reported as deceased, he merely looked them in the eye and asked if he resembled a corpse. Let me tell you, getting stared down by a witch made your blood run cold as ice, regardless of their spiritual status.

The guard at the Allwood's front gate admitted me, and I drove around the winding access road to the family's parking area. Jacob had been very grateful for my help—I had caught his murderer, after all—and as a result, I had full access to the family's compound. I didn't use that access for much, but it came in handy when I wanted to talk to Jacob while also avoiding his many-layered staff.

The truth was that I was grateful for Jacob's help as well. He'd helped me just as much as I'd helped him, maybe more so, and being that we hadn't met until after he was dead, he'd had no reason to do anything for the living. Most souls moved on once they died, regardless of their method of passing, but Jacob claimed he had unfinished business. It seemed like his business was to look out for his clan for the next hundred years or so, and I was fine with that.

I slipped into the estate through the kitchen door, crept through the corridors like a cat burglar, and found Jacob in his study. It resembled an old world gentleman's club, complete with oak paneling on the walls, leather armchairs, and a huge fireplace. The room was devoid of his staffers today, and the central air conditioning was cranked to Arctic levels, just the way I liked it.

Jacob Allwood was sitting behind his massive polished mahogany desk, which was probably worth more than my car. Today he was wearing a crisp white shirt rolled up at the sleeves, and his glasses perched on the tip of his nose. To his left sat a glass of Scotch, and on his right, a cigar smoldered away in an ashtray. He looked good for a dead man, and he knew it.

I knocked on the doorframe. "Afternoon, sir."

Jacob looked up and smiled. "Eli! When did you get here? The staff is supposed to announce visitors," he added, a bit miffed.

"I snuck in through the kitchen. Do you actually get a buzz off that?" I asked, nodding toward the Scotch.

"Sadly, no, but I can taste it."

Interesting. Jacob seemed to be capable of all sorts of things ordinary spirits couldn't manage. "Good thing you have expensive taste."

"Isn't it, though? But I doubt you came by to discuss the finer points of Scotch. What can I do for you?"

"I visited Jada earlier, and she remembered something from her possession. It's always been my understanding that those under a possession have no memory of what happened."

"That is my understanding, as well," he said. "If the possessed one was aware of what was happening... Firstly, that individual would need to be exceptionally strong minded. While I don't doubt Jada's capabilities, wasn't she a child when Sarah first possessed her?"

"Yeah, she was nine."

"Mm. Therefore, being that her mind wasn't yet fully developed, the odds of it being able to fight off an invading spirit are slim, to say the least. Besides, if she'd been strong enough to be aware of what was happening she could have suppressed Sarah and gotten help." He picked up his Scotch and swirled it in the glass. "What did she remember?"

"She thinks she had a boyfriend named Nathaniel."

"Oh, dear." Jacob set down the glass. "That does complicate things."

I sat in the armchair opposite his desk. "Tell me everything that could go wrong."

"The worst case scenario is a mortal with a witch's memories," he replied. "Mortals being exposed to the supernatural world isn't a bad thing in and of itself, however this mortal is in essence still a child. She may not have the skills or capabilities to understand that if she discusses these memories with other mortals, they may question her sanity."

"Out of one psychiatric facility, and into another," I muttered. "When you refer to Sarah's memories, how many of them could Jada conceivably have?"

"All of them."

"You mean, all of them from the time she was possessed, right?"

"No, I mean all five centuries' worth of them." Jacob leaned forward, and continued, "The reason why the host is suppressed during a possession is to keep their mind separate. If both minds are active, the memories of each person will commingle with the other. Therefore, if Jada wasn't fully suppressed, and her consciousness existed alongside Sarah's, she may know everything Sarah knows."

I flopped back in the chair. "Holy shit."

"Holy shit, indeed." Jacob poured a second Scotch and slid it toward me. "Should I make that a double?"

"A double might knock me out." I picked up the glass but didn't drink it. Liquor tended to mess with my seer abilities, so I avoided it. It also gave me a headache. "Wouldn't Sarah have realized Jada's mind was watching her?"

"Who's to say? Perhaps Jada was Sarah's first possession. It would explain why she possessed the wrong person." Jacob watched me. "Have you considered gently asking Jada for information on Nathaniel?"

"I have, even though it seems like a slimy thing to do. 'Hey, Jada, let's be friends. Tell me all about the creepy man that took care of you for twenty years.'" I set the glass on the desk. "Do you think Nathaniel knows?"

Jacob shrugged. "That man knows everything and nothing, sometimes at the very same time. I would not be surprised if he realized Sarah's mistake and was waiting for an opportune moment to turn things to his advantage."

Time... "Tessa thinks he may be using a time spell."

"Does she?" Jacob leaned back in his chair. "Exactly what gave her that idea?"

I told Jacob everything that happened at the Chinese restaurant, from the eerily empty restaurant to the falling knives, and to Tessa's finding of a packed business a few hours later.

"And those inside had no idea that they'd been gone?" Jacob asked.

"They claimed they opened up at nine, but we were inside the building half an hour later and it was empty." I glanced at the clock above the fireplace. "Would a time spell move the people from the restaurant, or Nathaniel?"

"Either, or both," Jacob replied. "More importantly, if he is using such an incantation, it is both rare and requires an immense amount of power. Nathaniel must have located a power source, and a repository."

"A repository for the power?"

"No, for the people moved. He would move them—or himself—out of one time and to the repository, and then he would move back to the same time. Once he completed whatever he wanted to do, he would move the people out of the repository and return them to the same moment. Those moved would never know what had happened."

"So he's got a temporal waiting room?"

Jacob smiled. "Yes, that is a good way to think about it." The clock chimed the hour, and Jacob glanced at his computer screen. "Eli, I have a meeting I must attend."

"Say no more," I said as I stood. "Thank you for your help, and the Scotch."

"You didn't even drink it."

"It's the thought that counts."

I left my ghost buddy to his meeting and took the servant's passage back to the kitchens. As I made my way through the compound, I thought about what Jacob had told me. Jada could have all of Sarah's memories, which means she would also know quite a bit about Nathaniel. I'd been at this too long, and knew Nathaniel too well, to assume he didn't already know that Jada was a liability. That meant Jada was a target, and it was up to me to protect her.

CHAPTER 5

THE GHOST GUYS

THE NEXT MORNING, I got up before the sun and ran while it was still dark and cool. I liked to get my run in every day regardless of the weather, and I was always challenging myself to increase my run times, and to run on different terrains. I had been chased many times in my life, by many types of creatures, so keeping up my endurance could be the difference between life and death, probably my own.

I got back to my apartment around six, showered, and took a nap. Two hours later my phone woke me. Of course, it was Dan.

"You hate letting me sleep," I said when I picked up.

"What was the name of the restaurant you and Tess were at yesterday?"

"Dim Sum Delight. Why?"

"I'm here now, with a cook who claims a magician abducted him and held him captive for a day."

I sat up and started putting on my shoes. "I'll be there in fifteen minutes."

Seventeen minutes after ending the call, I walked through Dim Sum Delight's front door. The restaurant's employees were huddled near the bar while several uniformed police officers surrounded a man dressed in a white tee, pants, and an apron; I assumed he was the cook Dan mentioned. The cook was obviously agitated, and several officers were trying to calm him down. Everyone else in the room was either mad, confused, or a little of both.

As I stood at the entrance, Jill Sanders, the police department's forensics specialist, spotted me. "Lyons is over there," she said, jerking her head toward the booths.

"Thanks."

I avoided as many people as I could while I crossed the lobby and found Dan leaning against a table while he watched the restaurant workers and police glare at each other. When he saw me, his shoulders sagged in relief. "Thank god you're here."

"This all seems," I cast a glance at the chaos in the front of the dining room, "not fun."

"It isn't. Let's take a walk."

I followed Dan through the kitchen, which was devoid of the falling knives and flaming columns from the day before, and out the back door into an alley. Based on the stench, that Dumpster hadn't been emptied this week. Or month.

"You got here fast," he said. "You drive?"

"I walked," I replied, not hiding my confusion. Dan knew I lived two blocks away, and he wasn't one to beat around the bush. "What's wrong?"

"This case, for one." He ran a hand through his hair and stared toward the alley's terminus in a parking lot. "I need to know what happened when you were here yesterday." He faced me, and added, "Everything that happened."

That look was code for "don't leave out the illegal bits", so I began with picking the lock, and ended with Tessa and me finding a random buckle. I even mentioned Tessa's suspicion that Nathaniel had used a time spell. "And you were there when I handed off the buckle to Bennet," I concluded.

"Yeah. I remember. Why were you here in the first place?"

"Tessa cast a divination spell, and she got this address," I replied. "It's how we've been tracking Nathaniel."

"Divination. I can't exactly work with that."

"You don't have to." Dan's frown became a scowl. "Let me and Tessa handle the magical side. You don't need to worry about that."

"That's just it," he snapped. I took a step back; Dan never snapped at anyone, not even criminals screaming in his face. He definitely never snapped at me. "I've got a man in there insisting he was kidnapped by a magician. I know he's legit, but I can't exactly write a report about how an evil witch moved him to a different time and place. What the hell am I supposed to do about that?"

I put my hand on his arm. "Take a breath. I freak out, not you, remember?"

He closed his eyes, and said, "I don't know what happened before you and Tess got here yesterday, but that cook was supposed to open the kitchen. When the owner arrived, and the cook wasn't here, he fired him. Now the cook is back, and claiming a magician kidnapped him."

"That's harsh, getting fired over one incident." Dan opened his eyes and let out an exasperated sigh. "I know. Not the point. Who called the cops?"

"The owner. The cook's refusing to leave until he gets his job back, pay for yesterday, justice against his kidnapper... It's a fricken' circus in there."

"It's okay. We've handled crazier."

"I guess we have." Dan closed his eyes again and let his head droop. He seemed exhausted, so I moved to steady him with an arm around his waist. He draped an arm around my shoulders and rested his forehead against the top of my head. We stood there for a moment, sharing each other's strength, and I remembered what Jacob had once called us: a circle unbroken.

"I'm sorry," Dan said. "I shouldn't be hanging all over you like this."

"It's okay," I said, when neither of us moved away. "I lean on you all the time. I can return the favor."

Dan lifted his head, then he stroked his hand over my cheek and tilted up my chin. "Yeah?"

"There she is!"

I looked past Dan toward the voice, and saw a trio of men wearing cargo shorts, fishing vests with many pockets, and backpacks bursting with cords and antennas. "Goddammit," I muttered.

"You know them?" Dan asked.

"Not them specifically, but they know me." I stepped back from Dan and steeled myself for the inevitable. "They're ghost hunters."

"For real? Like on TV?" Dan asked, then the guys were standing in front of us.

"Eliza Moore, the legend," one of the men said. "We're big fans."

"Of my detective work?" I asked hopefully. "And, how did you find me?"

"We went by your office, but it was closed," he replied. "We used our ghost detector, and it led us right to you!"

"Ghost... detector?" I asked.

"The finest in the business," he replied, then he showed me a modified transistor radio. "Gary made it." One of the others—presumably Gary—raised his hand.

"Great," I said. "Well, I'm in the middle of something—"

"With ghosts? We can help!"

"And you are?" Dan demanded, putting his hand on his hip, thus revealing his badge and gun.

"I'm Mike Delacorte," he replied. "And we are the Ghost Guys. You've probably heard of our podcast."

"I haven't," Dan said. "We're in the middle of an investigation, so if you'll all just move along, that would be great." When the Ghost Guys stood there staring at us, Dan added, "If you don't leave, *now*, I can arrest each one of you for interference."

"Okay, okay," Mike said, raising his hands as he backed away. "Eliza, can we meet up later?"

"She's busy," Dan barked, then he herded me down the alley and toward the front door of the restaurant.

"Normally, I would be really irritated if you spoke for me, but that was okay," I said. "Could you really arrest them?"

"Probably not," he admitted. "Have you worked with ghost hunters in the past?"

"All I've ever done is send them packing." I shook out my hands; even though most ghost hunters were harmless, I did not like dealing with them. "A few years ago, someone broke into a shepherd's house and stole a list of names and addresses of active seers. At the time, no one thought it was a big deal, because seers aren't exactly in hiding. Then some fool posted the list on the internet, and every paranormal enthusiast in the country decided that working with a seer was the best way to track down ghosts."

"That's got to be annoying," Dan said, and I nodded. "How often do they come by?"

"I've never seen those three before," I replied. "Every so often a few ghost hunters come by my office, but I lock the door and pretend I'm closed."

"Do they go to your grandmother's house?"

"No. The shepherd in question had her name, but not her address." Gran was so well known in the seer world that if you needed her, you knew how to find her. Or, she would find you. "Good thing, too. If one of them stopped by, my dad would have flipped."

"He a violent guy?"

"No, but he'll do anything to protect his family."

"Can't argue with that." Dan opened the door, and we reentered the front of the restaurant. In stark contrast to what had been happening ten minutes ago, no one was arguing. The restaurant workers were prepping to open, while the police stood around looking dumfounded.

"And now everyone's getting along," I said. "Weird."

"Weirder, you mean." Dan beckoned Jill over. "Exactly what changed in the last few minutes?"

"As you know, the cook was adamant he shouldn't be fired," she began, "but the owner was furious when he wasn't here yesterday. Apparently, they have a love-hate relationship." Something crashed in the kitchen, followed by shouting. "Maybe it's more hate than love."

"So, the owner changed his mind on firing the cook?" Dan asked.

"No, the cook challenged the owner to a contest," she replied. "They're having a cook-off."

"A... cook-off?" I repeated.

"Yep. They're both preparing the same dishes. If the cook's is better, he gets to keep his job with yesterday's pay."

"And if the owner wins?"

"I think the cook gets to keep his job, but with no back pay," Jill replied.

Dan clapped his hands. "All right. Seems like we can go."

"Or we could stay and ask the cook a few more questions," I said. When Jill glared at me, I continued, "What if he really was kidnapped?"

"Doubtful," she said.

"Listen, if you and the rest want to take off, it's fine," Dan said. "I'll stay and talk to the guy."

"Earlier you were about to blow your top. Now you want to hang around?" Jill shook her head. "I don't know what you said to him, Eli, but write it down so I can use it?"

"I just reminded Detective Lyons of his gentle nature," I said. Jill laughed as Dan shook his head, then she went to speak to the rest of the officers.

Dan and I took a seat at the bar. Through the service window, we could see the cook and the owner at the prep table, chopping vegetables and measuring ingredients. "They work well together," I observed.

"You think he'll give you anything on Beauclaire?" Dan asked, jerking his chin toward the cook.

"Can't hurt to ask," I replied. "Besides, he wants to talk. We might as well listen."

The owner saw us through the service window and barked a few orders. A moment later, the hostess brought us plates and cutlery.

"We're just here to interview the cook," Dan said, but she was undeterred.

"If you sit, you eat," she said. "Tea?"

"Yes, please," I said. The hostess went to get our tea. Dan looked at me and cocked an eyebrow. "Hey, if they want to feed us, I'm game. I haven't had breakfast yet."

Dan blew out a breath and rubbed his eyes. "I have never had Chinese food for breakfast. I didn't even know that was a thing."

"What do you think people do in China? Starve until noon?"

He peeked at me over his hand, the corner of his mouth curled up. "Are you ever not a smartass?"

"Never."

Our breakfast of champions turned out to be an assortment of steamed dumplings, and they were delicious. Apparently they were so delicious that the cook and owner mended fences while they made the dumplings, and by the time we'd finished eating everyone was friendly again.

After Dan and I were finished with breakfast, the cook came out to talk to us. He sat behind the bar, facing us with an unlit cigarette in his hand. I noticed how his hands trembled.

"Want to talk about it?" I asked. "What happened yesterday, I mean."

"You believe me?" he asked. "I don't need anyone making fun of me. I get enough of that from him," he added, his gaze sliding toward the owner.

"We believe something happened to you," Dan said. "Tell us your side of the story."

He tapped the cigarette on the bar. "I'm always the first one here," he began. "Before the deliveries start unloading, before anyone. I don't need to get in so early, but I like to set up my kitchen a certain way, you know? So I was here, and I hadn't even turned the lights on yet, and I heard a man's voice."

"What part of the restaurant were you in?" Dan asked.

"In the stockroom," he replied. "The voice came from the kitchen. I stopped what I was doing and went to the kitchen. I figured I forgot to lock the door and someone wandered in, thinking we were open."

"Did you get a good look at him?"

"When I came into the kitchen, his back was to me. The lights were still off, but sunlight was coming in through the back door. He was tall, thin. Gray clothes, I think, and a hat. No bright colors."

"What was he doing?" I asked.

"Standing in the middle of the room, leaning on the counter," he replied.

"He wasn't doing anything with his hands, or talking?" I pressed.

He shook his head. "He was still as a statue. Then he spun around, and just like that," he snapped his fingers, "I was in a dark room."

"You mean he shut the door, and that made it dark in the kitchen?" Dan asked.

"No, I was sent to a dark room that wasn't part of this restaurant," he replied. "It had stone walls, and a dirt floor. It was damp, and gross, and I was there until this morning when I appeared back in the kitchen like nothing ever happened. I thought it was all a dream, until this asshole tried firing me," he added, nodding toward the owner.

"He was probably just worried about you, after you went missing yesterday," I said.

He ducked his head, blushing. "Yeah. Maybe."

"If you don't mind, I'd like you to come down to the station and talk to our sketch artist." Dan handed his card to the cook. "If we can get an image of this guy circulating, maybe we can catch him before he tries this on anyone else."

"You really believe me," the cook said, staring from me to Dan. "I figured you were gonna lock me up."

"Why wouldn't we believe you?" I asked. "Obviously, something happened to you, and even if that man isn't responsible, he has vital information. He's our prime suspect, right, Detective?"

Dan's gaze slid toward me. "Correct, Miss Moore. We'll get out of your hair now, but definitely come by the station. What do I owe you for our breakfast?"

CHAPTER 6

ROSEMARY, THAT'S FOR REMEMBRANCE

"Pretty slick, getting the cook to talk to the sketch artist," I said, as Dan and I left the restaurant.

"Why, thank you," Dan said. "I figure if we get Beauclaire's image circulating—assuming the person this guy saw really was Beauclaire—maybe we can get ahead of him, for once."

"We can only hope." We emerged from the alley into the parking lot, and I remembered I hadn't taken my car to the restaurant. "Oh, I walked. I'll talk to you later."

"Eli," Dan called, and I turned back to him. "I have some information about the halfway house Jada's assigned to."

"Really? Is it a good place?"

"On paper, yes, but there's something weird about it." He rubbed the back of his neck. "I started a file, if you want to have a look."

"Okay. Is it at the station?"

"It's at my place."

I stopped short. "Oh."

"We can go look at it. If you want to, that is. I mean, I don't want you to think I'm trying to get you over to my place for anything other than work."

I smiled, because a flustered, stammering Dan Lyons was just about the cutest thing in the galaxy. "I wouldn't think that. Besides, you're at my apartment all the time."

"Well, it's your office, too." He glanced at his car. "We can go now, if you have time."

"Sure."

We got in the car, and Dan pulled out of the parking lot. As for me, I kept my face turned toward the side window. Not only did I already know his address, I was beyond excited, since I was finally going to see where he lived.

After a few minutes, Dan turned down a tree-lined street. The houses were spaced a good distance apart, the yards were neat, and the entire street looked like something out of a fifties sitcom. As I marveled at the perfect family oriented neighborhood, Dan pulled into the driveway of a good sized brick house. It had two stories, big, beautiful windows, and a well-maintained and spacious yard.

"This is where you live?" I blurted out.

"Yeah. Why? What's wrong with it?"

I stared at the house that was perfect for a family to grow up in. "By yourself?"

"Were you expecting my college roommate to be hanging around? Yes, by myself." Dan got out of the car, and I followed.

"It's kind of big for just you." I peeked into the backyard. It was gorgeous. "Do you at least have a dog?"

"I'm not home enough for a dog," he replied. "And it's not that big."

"Bet you've never said that before."

Dan glanced at me over his shoulder, the smirkiest of smirks on his face. That was it, the teasing was on. He put his hand on the front doorknob when something above us let out a screeching wail. I looked up and saw a two foot long slug-like creature, its mouth packed with concentric rings of sharp, yellowed teeth.

"It's a demon," I yelled, since nothing that ugly came from this realm. "Get back!"

The slug threw itself at us as we danced backward. I held my tattooed forearm above my head; it wasn't much protection, but it was all I had. Dan grabbed his gun and shot the slug, spattering goo everywhere.

"Is it dead?" I asked. I lowered my arm and grimaced. We were both covered in slug guts.

"It exploded on contact," Dan said. "Come on, let's get this shit off of us."

He turned to the door and fumbled with the keys. By the time we were inside, we learned what the slug's last line of defense was: not only did its flesh stink like a week-old corpse, its acidic blood was eating through our clothes and burning our skin.

"Shower," I said, rather desperately.

"Yeah." Dan stood in the center of the foyer, his head turning left and right. He pointed down the hall and yelled, "This way!"

I followed him into a tiled bathroom, both of us ripping off our slug-soaked clothing along the way. Dan flung open the shower door, turned on the water and we got in, neither of us caring that the water was icy cold. I stood under the showerhead, rinsing out my hair while Dan used the hand spray. As soon as the guts were gone, the burning sensation halted, and I didn't seem to have any marks on my skin. Nothing like a bit of good news after a demon attack. I turned toward Dan to share my discovery and froze.

I was in the shower with Dan, and we were both completely, totally naked.

We stared at each other for a moment, then he grabbed a blue bottle from the shelf. "Shampoo?"

"Thank you." I took the bottle and turned around, then I squirted out some shampoo and worked it into my hair. The liquid was slick, and it didn't lather. "I think this is conditioner."

"Sorry." Dan turned the sprayer on me and rinsed out the conditioner. I should have told him to stop, step back, or rinsed my own damn hair. I didn't do any of those things. I liked that he was helping me, and the way his fingers gently parted my hair and caressed my neck. I'd been pushing Dan away for so long, I almost forgot how much I enjoyed being near him.

When he finished rinsing my hair, he put the sprayer aside and set his hands on my waist.

"Is this okay?" he asked.

"Um, yeah. It's fine."

He slid his hands forward and embraced me from behind. I leaned back into him, letting him hold me up while the now-warm water cascaded over us. My eyes fluttered closed, and I imagined we were some place warm and tropical, and far away from ghosts and demon slugs and the rest of our problems. I felt his body harden behind me, but before I could react, his hand slid lower.

"Tell me if you want me to stop," he whispered. I nodded, but remained silent. He took my silence as an invitation and probed lower, gently stroking me. He found what he was searching for soon enough and I came hard, my hands pressed against the shower door while I rode his hand.

Dan held me for a moment, then he shut off the water and opened the shower door. He wrapped me in a towel and took my hand and led me to bed. We tumbled onto the mattress just as my adrenaline bottomed out. I was asleep before my head hit the pillow.

When I opened my eyes, Dan's face was mere inches from mine, and he was staring at me. That was disconcerting.

"Hi," he said.

"Hi."

My memories came rushing back: the demon attack, Dan shooting it—holy shit, what must his neighbors be thinking—then the shower... and what had happened in the shower. That had been inappropriate and unprofessional and awesome.

Wait, what was that last part?

"You okay?" he asked.

"I'm fine." I thought about the shower incident and felt my face warm. "I'm good."

"Good."

He smiled, then he slid down the bed, pushed open my thighs and kissed me. I could get used to this inappropriate and unprofessional behavior.

After Dan made me come a second time, he sat back on his heels and watched me writhing in aftershocks. Once they'd subsided, I raised myself up on my elbows and regarded him, naked and kneeling at the edge of the bed.

"I feel like I owe you," I said, then I repositioned myself and took him in my mouth. He didn't protest, and let me show him how much I appreciated his efforts.

After a few minutes, I noticed that he wasn't making any sounds, not even little grunts of enjoyment, nor was he moving. I glanced upward and saw him staring out the bedroom door.

"Dan?"

He looked down at me. "Yeah?"

I sat up. "Are you all right?"

"Yeah." He got up and opened a dresser drawer, then pulled on a tee shirt. "I'm going to the kitchen."

"Um, okay."

He grabbed a pair of boxers and left the bedroom. I sat there on the bed, confused as hell. He hadn't even come, and in all my days I'd never known a man who didn't react in the slightest to getting a blow job. What's more, now that I thought about it, he hadn't really been affectionate with me, he'd just zeroed in on my erogenous zones and made me come. Twice. Dan Lyons had been trying to distract me with orgasms.

Crap. He was possessed.

How was I so certain that Dan was possessed? He hadn't been affectionate with me.

Dan was one of the most touchy feely people I've ever met. A baby would touch things, even going so far as to put things into their mouth, in order to learn more about their environment, and that was Dan. He had no qualms about touching evidence at a crime scene if he thought the tactile sensations could somehow offer up a clue.

Not only that, he was constantly lending me a hand or otherwise initiating contact between us. We'd walked hand-in-hand, held each other, and there was that time we made out like horny teenagers. Earlier he hadn't kissed me at all, not once in the shower, or afterward in bed. And once we got to bed, he hadn't even put his arms around me.

It all boiled down to this: Dan touched me all the time, so why would we have hardly any contact while we were in bed together?

Because there was a demon riding Dan, that's why. I suspected that the demon didn't feel physical sensations, as if its connection to the host was somehow incomplete. It was directing Dan's body, yes, but it was unable to feel pleasure. That would explain why Dan hadn't reacted when I'd turned the tables on him. His physical body was getting aroused just fine, but the sensations weren't traveling to the demon's awareness. While I'd been on my knees with his cock in my mouth, the demon had been impatiently waiting for me to finish.

I flopped back onto the bed and sighed. Just an average day in my humiliating life.

But wallowing wouldn't help me or Dan. I got off the bed and raided the closet for a tee shirt and some sweatpants, then I followed Demon Dan into the kitchen. He—or rather, his body—was standing at the counter, staring out of the window into the backyard. I wondered what the demon was looking for—or maybe waiting for—and decided I didn't want to find out. I needed to get this entity out of Dan's body, fast, and get his spirit back where it belonged.

Trapped.

The room swayed, and I grabbed the doorjamb for support. It had been months since I'd last had a flashback to when I'd been kidnapped as a teen, and one chose this moment to smack me upside my head. I concentrated on the sound of the clock ticking, the feel of the cool tile floor underneath my feet, and forced my panic attack to subside.

There would be time for panicking later. Right now, Dan needed me.

I glanced around the kitchen, mentally cataloging what I had to work with. I needed to counteract this possession, fast, but I had a feeling that Dan didn't keep a cabinet of demon banishing supplies close at hand. Since I couldn't search through the house without arousing suspicion, I came up with a plan on the fly.

"I bet you're hungry," I said. "Let's make something to eat."

Demon Dan's mouth stretched, and I saw his teeth; a beat too late, I realized that was supposed to be a smile. I suppressed a shudder and opened the fridge. There were eggs and milk, good for eating but not for repelling demons. I brought the eggs to the stove and rummaged around for pans. In the cabinet next to the stove, I found a container of salt. Finally, something useful.

I set the entire canister of salt on the counter and put a frying pan on the stove. If worse came to worst, I could always smack him on the head with the pan. I continued my sweep of the kitchen and saw a set of four herbs in pots perched on the windowsill. Because Dan was terminally cheesy, the herbs were parsley, sage, rosemary, and thyme, just like the song.

Rosemary, that's for remembrance.

Okay, that was a line from Shakespeare, and not a magical instruction. Still, I had to work with what was available. I yanked off a few springs of rosemary and set them in a bowl. Next, I poured out enough salt to cover the sprigs. Once that was done, I stood perfectly still and waited for my moment.

Demon Dan finished staring at whatever was so interesting out back and sat at the kitchen table. The demon clearly didn't see me as a threat, since it kept its back to me. Still, Dan was bigger and a lot stronger than me. I needed to approach the demon carefully, or I could end up worse off that Dan.

"Can you crack these eggs for me?" I asked. I set the carton of eggs and an empty bowl in front of him.

"Sure."

Demon Dan set about cracking eggs. After he'd done the third egg, I threw my left arm around his neck in a choke hold and shoved the bowl of salt and rosemary into his face.

Dan bellowed and threw his weight back. I danced out of the way as he crashed to the floor, chair and all. I leapt onto his chest and poured more salt onto his face, then I pressed the rest of the rosemary against his forehead.

"I cast you out," I said. I drew upon my seer's abilities, yanking power from the depths of my bones as I pulled the entity out of Dan and shoved it away. "Demon, return from whence you came!"

Dan bucked his hips, and I became acutely aware that the only things separating me from him were my thin sweatpants and his thinner boxers. I kept pouring salt onto his face until his mouth was full. When the canister was empty, I covered his mouth and nose with my hands, and hoped I'd get the demon to leave before I did any permanent harm to Dan.

Eventually, Dan's chest ballooned and then collapsed. His eyes watered and went bloodshot, then his whole body went limp. I removed my hand from his mouth and patted his cheek.

"Dan? Dan!" I brushed the salt off his face, and then cradled his head in my hands, drawing up the last of my reserves as I desperately tried to pull his spirit back to his body. "Dan, please. Come back to me." He remained still as a statue, and I lost whatever shreds of calm I had left. "Dan, please," I pleaded. "Don't leave me."

"Eli," he rasped, his mouth and throat parched from the salt. I leapt up and got him a glass of water. He sat up and drank some water, then he washed out his mouth and spat onto the floor.

"Is it really you?" I asked.

"Yeah. I was in a place, someplace dark..." He shook his head. "Was I in hell?"

"You were possessed," I said. "That's why your mouth is full of salt. I had to get the spirit out of you."

Dan spat again, then he drank the rest of the water. "You saved me?"

"I got you back. I'm sorry it took so long—"

He dropped the empty glass and pulled me into his arms. "Thank you, babe. You saved me. Thank you so much."

Chapter 7

Dialed Up To Eleven

Since Dan was all wet and salty, he went off to change while I cleaned up the kitchen. There wasn't much to clean, just some salt to sweep up and eggs to send down the drain. Once that was done, I left the kitchen but stopped short of entering the bedroom. After what had happened between me, Dan's body, and an entity that may or may not have been a demon, I didn't want to ever set foot in there again.

Before I could figure out a reason to get out of his house and never return, Dan called out to me.

"Eli?"

"Yeah?"

"Can, um... Can you come in here?"

I wanted to say no, but the waver in Dan's voice told me how much he needed me. "I'm coming in."

Steeling myself, I entered the bedroom and found Dan standing in front of the adjacent bathroom door. He was staring at a heap of rags on the floor. After a moment, I realized that those rags were what was left of our clothes.

"What is this mess?" he asked.

"Those are our clothes," I replied. "After you shot the demon—"

"I shot something?" Panicked, Dan looked around the room. "Where's my gun?"

"I-I don't know."

Dan turned in a circle, his hands on his head, then he made a beeline for the area behind the door. His gun was wedged in the corner as if it had skidded across the floor. He picked it up, checked it, then he set it on top of his dresser.

"Never in my life have I left a gun on the floor. Any floor," he added. "I... I shot something? Where?"

"A demon attacked us on your front walk."

He barreled past me toward the front door and flung it open. When I caught up to him, he was standing on his front step, his head swinging from side to side as he surveyed his yard.

"When did this happen?" he asked.

"A few hours ago," I replied. "We came back here after interviewing the cook at the Chinese restaurant, and before we got inside—"

"That was hours ago?" He looked at his watch. "If I discharged my weapon out here, in my front yard in broad daylight, where are the cops? No one called 911? Why aren't my neighbors freaking out?" He stepped closer and asked, "Where's the body?"

"Let's get inside." Dan let me lead him inside the house. I shut the door, and said, "You should probably lie down."

"I'm not a baby," he bit off.

"No, you're not, but you just had a demon controlling you for the last," I glanced at the clock on the living room's wall, "eight hours." I blinked, and looked at the clock again. I didn't feel like I'd slept for that long, but what with Dan's possession, I'd probably lost track of time. "Possessions are hard on mortal bodies, and you need to recover."

"Eight... eight hours." Dan covered his face with his hands. "What the hell happened to me?" It broke my heart to see him in so much emotional pain, and that wasn't even taking into account what he must be feeling physically.

"Get in bed," I said. "I'll bring you some water. Are you hungry?"

"I think I might throw up."

"Just water, then." I went into the kitchen and filled a glass from the pitcher in the fridge. When I returned to the bedroom, Dan was sitting on the bed, leaning against the headboard. I handed him the water, then I sat at the foot of the bed.

"I don't know why no one called the police," I began. "Honestly, I didn't even think about it at the time. The demon came from above, you shot it, and we ran inside." I looked at his gun, lying on the dresser. It looked like a regular gun, not a demon killing weapon. "Will you have to account for the missing bullet?"

"I'm more concerned with where that bullet ended up." He eyed my shirt. "You're wearing my clothes."

"Mine are there," I said, nodding toward the heap of slimy fabric. "When you shot the demon, it exploded, and its guts were caustic. It ate through our clothes."

"Glad I don't remember that," he muttered. "I think I was where the cook was."

"The cook—oh, in that room he mentioned?"

Dan nodded. "It was cold, and dark, and no matter how much I screamed, no one heard me. No one came." He cleared his throat and dragged the back of his hand across his cheek. "No one heard me."

"Who were you yelling for?"

"You. I called for you." Dan fixed me in his gaze, and I saw how frightened he'd really been. "You say it was eight hours, but it felt like eight thousand years. I was terrified they had you, too, that you were stuck in a different room... All I could think about was how scared you must be, all alone in the dark. I kept yelling your name, but you didn't hear me."

I moved to the top of the bed and sat next to him. After a moment, he turned into me and I held him, just like how Gran used to hold me when I was small and scared. "I heard you. Maybe not with my ears, but I heard you. I wasn't going to let them keep you. Even if the salt and rosemary hadn't worked, I wouldn't have stopped until I got you back."

Dan nestled himself against me, his head tucked underneath my chin. "I don't know what I'd do without you, Eli."

It wasn't long until Dan was asleep, which I thought was for the best. What with how long his consciousness had been trapped in that small, dark place, he needed psychic rest as much as physical.

I watched Dan for a little while before I left. He looked younger, sleep having softened the lines of his face. I realized that I didn't actually know how old Dan was, not that it mattered, but for the first time, I wondered if we were closer in age than I realized.

Not that it mattered.

I scooped our ruined clothes into a garbage bag and tossed it into the outdoor trash. Hopefully, whatever was left of the slug wouldn't eat through the trash can. I let myself out of Dan's house and did a cursory investigation of his front yard. I didn't find a spent shell casing anywhere, but then again, I wasn't familiar enough with firearms to know if they really left empty bullets lying around, or if that was just in the movies. Either way, Dan was right; it was downright odd that no one in this family friendly neighborhood had called the police upon hearing a gunshot. Or seeing a demon slug.

In a supreme stroke of luck, I'd left my bag with my phone and keys inside Dan's car, and said car was unlocked. Not a very safe practice, but it did mean my bag was free of demon guts. I grabbed my bag and started walking home. It took me almost an hour to get to my apartment, which left me plenty of time to think.

Tessa had suspected that Nathaniel Beauclaire had used a time spell at the restaurant, and that was how he had evaded us. I wondered if the demon could have used a similar time spell in Dan's yard, so no one heard or saw what happened. That would also account for our missing eight hours. I didn't know very much about demons, but I'd always been under the impression that they didn't wield magic. Rather, they got wielded by witches, almost like hired muscle. If that was true, it meant that a witch saw Dan as enough of a threat to conjure a demon and leave it in his front yard.

There was also the unavoidable coincidence between what had happened to Dan and the cook from Dim Sum Delight. Both Dan and the cook had described being trapped in a small, dark space. I wondered if Jada had been stuck in such a space for the last twenty years. Since wondering wouldn't help anyone, as soon as I was inside my apartment I called the one person who always knew the answers to all my questions, or how to find them: our local shepherd, Bennet Carrington.

"Eli," Bennet greeted. "Are you calling to follow up on the buckle?"

"No, not the buckle. How much do you know about possessions? Specifically, demon possessions?"

"I am quite knowledgeable on the subject," he replied. "They are similar to any other possession, though a demonic possession does tend to be rather rough on the victim."

I recalled Dan's exhaustion, the dark smudges underneath his eyes. "What happens to the possessed person's mind? Does it go dormant, the way Jada's should have when she was possessed by Sarah Allwood?"

"That is the major difference. A human and a demonic consciousness cannot occupy the same space, so the host's mind must be sent out, almost like an astral projection."

So the cook and Dan were both possessed by demons. "How do demons find their marks? Do they just hang out looking for interesting bodies to hop into?"

"Generally speaking, demons want very little to do with the mortal world," Bennet replied. "They can be conjured and enthralled by witches, but it requires a vast expenditure of power." Bennet paused and asked, "Has someone been possessed?"

"Even better, I think the same demon may have possessed two different people." I paused, for once unwilling to share the whole story with Bennet. I felt like it was Dan's choice to share his possession with others, not mine, and I was going to respect his privacy. "So, did you learn anything about the buckle?"

"A bit, but nothing that will assist us in locating Nathaniel Beauclaire," he replied. "The buckle is of a style and age that could have been worn by him in his younger days, when he first arrived in this country."

"You're saying it could be Nathaniel's personal property?"

"It's a possibility, although why he would have left it in a restaurant is a mystery I've yet to solve. I will keep digging."

"Thank you, Bennet."

I ended the call, then I held my head in my hands as memories of those hours with the demon came rushing back to me. I'd thought I was with Dan, not just his body, but all of him. I hadn't shied away from him in the shower, or in bed, and damn it all, I enjoyed it. I enjoyed being with Dan, and when I'd woken up in bed with him, I was happy. Confused as hell and wondering if any of this was a good idea, but very, very happy.

Now the truth was out, and while I was glad to have the real Dan back, I'd also dialed my confusion up to eleven. He had no memory of what happened while he was possessed; in his mind, we'd still only kissed that one time, and that was months ago. The only two who knew what really happened were me and the demon. What's worse, I'd exorcised that demon, but I hadn't destroyed it. What if it possessed Dan again?

What if this demon had ruined any chance I'd ever had with Dan before I ever figured out if I wanted to be with him?

Chapter 8

The Apples Are Rotting

Since I'd spent the bulk of yesterday with Dan, both the original and demonic versions, the next day was all about client work. This was made clear when I returned to my apartment after my morning run and found Tessa sitting at my kitchen table.

"Morning," I said. "Have you been here long?"

"Just long enough to look over the schedule." Tessa paused, and nibbled a pastry. Being that she didn't gain weight or suffer other ill effects from a diet heavy in fat and sugar, she always had a supply of baked goods nearby. "Dan called."

I stopped moving. "He called the office line? Why didn't he call my cell?"

"That, I don't know. What I do know is that the restaurant cook you and he interviewed yesterday was spotted on a few surveillance cameras doing a few awkward things while he claimed he was possessed." Tessa pulled out the chair next to her. "Why don't you sit and have some coffee, and tell me what happened between you and Detective Lyons."

"Nothing happened," I said too quickly. When Tessa quirked an eyebrow, I collapsed into the chair next to her. "Seriously. Nothing happened with Dan, but there was a demon that things did happen to. With." I took a deep breath. "Dan got possessed, probably by the same demon that possessed the cook."

"This was the cook from the restaurant we went to?"

"Yes."

"Hmm." Tessa tapped her chin. "If we're now dealing with demonic possessions, I wonder if any of this is related to Nathaniel."

"If not Nathaniel, then who?" I asked. "Who or what would want to possess a cook, and then Dan?"

Tessa picked out a croissant from the bakery box and set it in front of me. "That one has chocolate. Start from the beginning."

I did as ordered and relayed everything that happened the day before, starting with Dan calling me from the restaurant, and ending with me walking home wearing Dan's clothes. By the time I was done, I'd shredded the croissant to crumbs and Tessa's eyes were wide as saucers.

"You just hopped into the shower," Tessa said. "With Dan."

"You would fixate on that." I scraped some of the crumbs into my hand, got up, and tossed them into the sink. "There were demon guts everywhere. We had to wash it off."

"Whatever possessed Dan wasn't the same demon he shot," she said. "For the body to be obliterated the way you describe, the mind would have died as well. The slug was likely a distraction."

"Well, it worked. We were plenty distracted." I reclaimed my seat. "So? What do I do?"

"About what? The demon?"

"That, and Dan... and everything." I folded my arms on the table and laid my head on top of them. "Dan has literally no memory of what happened, but I can't stop thinking about it."

"No, he wouldn't have any memories, other than of wherever his consciousness was sent." Tessa smoothed my hair back from my face. "What can I do for you? How can I help?"

I extended my arm across the table, and Tessa grasped my hand. For as long as I could remember, Tessa and I had a very specific agreement. When we were holding hands, we could tell each other anything without judgement or repercussions.

"I have thought about being with Dan dozens of times," I began. "Maybe hundreds. What happened yesterday wasn't anything like what I imagined."

"Was he too rough?"

"He was barely anything. There was hardly any affection. It was like he just wanted to get it over with."

"It wasn't really Dan," Tessa soothed. "Dan is quite fond of you. You know that."

"What if he's not? What if he never was, and it was all in my head, and now after this he wants nothing to do with me?"

"Do you want to have something with him?"

"I don't know. I really don't. But I don't like that this demon might have taken it from me before I got a chance to decide. It's not fair."

"Life isn't fair. Sometimes, it's downright awful. But the demon is gone and you're still here, and Dan's still here. That means you still have a chance."

"A chance at what?"

"That's for you to figure out."

After Tessa finished grilling me for minute details of what had happened between me and Demon Dan—really, who cares about manscaping?—I showered and changed, and Nine Lives Investigations opened for business. Our first two appointments were standard background checks; boring, but they would pay the bills. The third appointment was with a Mike Delacorte.

"This name sounds familiar," I said to Tess. "When did he make this appointment?"

"Yesterday, while you were off," Tessa began, then she fluttered her hand. Apparently that was sign language for "dealing with a demon possession". "He said you two met yesterday morning."

"We did?" I mentally ran down the list of everyone I interacted with yesterday, and realized who this person was. "Crap. He's a ghost hunter."

"You're joking. What does he think he'll accomplish with this appointment?"

"No idea. I hope he brings his ghost equipment. It's hilarious."

Three o'clock rolled around, and Mike Delacorte arrived right on time. He strode through the door and looked around the office like a kid in a candy store, grinning at random things like the coat rack and the back of my monitor. "Hey, Eliza. Wow, your office is great. Hey," he said to Tessa, extending his arm for a handshake. "I'm Mike Delacorte, the Ghost Guy."

Tessa looked at his hand as if it was a bug. "Lovely. Why do you find yourself in need of our services? Are the ghosts refusing to play nicely with you?"

Mike laughed. Tessa didn't. "I needed to talk to Eliza, and scheduling time in the office seemed like the best way to do it. You seemed pretty irritated when we came up to you in the alley."

"Astute deduction," I said. That was probably the only astute deduction he'd made this week. "The rate is seventy-five dollars per hour, and the clock started ticking the moment you walked in. What would you like to discuss?"

Mike seemed a bit taken aback, as if he'd assumed we'd casually talk shop for a few minutes instead of getting right to work. "We've been tracking ghost signatures," he began. "They were very strong at the restaurant yesterday. I'm sure you noticed."

"Exactly how does one track a ghost?" Tessa asked.

Mike gave Tessa some side eye. "Is she new at this?" he asked me.

"I haven't been new at anything for a very, very long time," Tessa said. "Please answer the question."

Mike glanced between Tessa and me. "Who's in charge around here?"

"We are, and you're not," I said. After a brief staring match, Mike raised his hands in defeat.

"Okay, okay. Gary modified a few transistor radios to pick up paranormal frequencies. Those are the ghost detectors. We used them to track some weird frequencies toward their origin point, and that led us to the restaurant."

Behind Mike, Tessa mouthed "paranormal frequencies". I tried not to laugh, and asked, "Do you have one of these detectors on you?"

"Always do." Mike pulled out a small gray device from one of his many vest pockets. It had a dial, a headset, and two knobs that looked like they controlled volume. All in all this ghost detector was a dead ringer for my dad's vintage eighties Walkman.

There was a metal plate on the floor underneath my desk, which was original to the building. I had no idea as to its purpose, but whenever I tapped it three times my best undead friend, Prudence, appeared. I tapped the plate now with the toe of my boot, and she was in the room within seconds. Prudence frowned—she didn't like being summoned—and quickly sized up Mike.

"Who is this fool?" she demanded.

I held up my hand, and asked Mike, "Are there any ghosts here with us now?"

Mike fiddled with the knobs of the ghost detector, then declared, "Nope, only us living folks."

Prudence sniffed. "Imbecile."

"You're not wrong," I said to Prudence. Mike, assuming I was speaking to him, grinned. "Thanks for the demonstration. Exactly what does all of this high-tech gadgetry have to do with me?"

"We thought you could maybe use some help, you know, tracking down the entities you're hunting," he replied. "We're here to offer our services to the legendary Eliza Moore."

"First of all, how do you even know who I am?" I glanced at Tessa. She shrugged. "I'm a private investigator, not a ghost hunter."

"But you use ghosts on your cases," he said, and I shook my head.

"I am hired by living people, and I investigate living people. Seems like you're the victim of misinformation."

Mike frowned. "Um, yeah. I guess so. What do I owe you for the session?"

"It's on me. Have a good day."

It took him a moment to realize he'd been dismissed, then Mike stood and left my office. He hadn't been in my office for five minutes, yet he left me with a throbbing headache.

"That was nuts," I said. "Who tracks ghosts with a transistor radio?"

"That man wasn't tracking anything," Prudence said. "In my day, we called it selling snake oil."

Tessa watched the door for a moment, almost as if she was considering going after Mike. "What if they were tracking you?"

"Me? Why would they be tracking me?"

"I don't know, but for someone who was so eager to speak with you, he gave up rather easily." Tessa locked the front door. "There's also the matter of the possessions."

"What about them?"

"How many demonic possessions have you encountered in your life? Two, both within the past few days. I've lived a lot longer that you have, and I haven't encountered more than ten. That's odd." Tessa sat in the chair Mike had vacated. "And, as you pointed out, how do these Ghost Guys even know who you are?"

"He never answered that, did he?" I opened a new browser window on my laptop. "I think it's time to investigate these ghost hunters."

"Before you do that, I've news on the orchard," Prudence said. She'd been hanging around Stone Creek Orchard at my request, keeping a ghostly eye out for Sarah Allwood's spirit. "The apples are rotting."

"Are they?" Since they'd ripened in April, and no one had harvested them, I supposed it made sense that they were rotting a few months later. "Is that bad?"

"It's unprecedented," Prudence said. "Those apples have always been ripe for picking, no matter the season. Something has happened to alter the very fabric of the orchard."

I looked at Tessa. "Could it be Sarah?"

"If the orchard was somehow linked to Sarah's spirit, it's a possibility," Tessa said. "You still haven't come across any hint of her in the spirit realm?"

"I have not," Prudence replied. "I shall continue to watch for the she-devil, and I will keep you apprised of any new developments at the orchard."

"Interesting," I said, after Prudence dissipated. "Maybe Sarah's spirit moved on."

"Perhaps, but I don't think we should assume as much," Tessa said. "Sarah is a wild card. We must proceed as if she's still a threat, although," she cast another glance at the closed door, "the Ghost Guys do appear to be the more pressing problem."

I sighed, and went back to my internet search. "Great. Just great."

Chapter 9

Right Next To My Plaster Cast Of Bigfoot

Tessa left around six, but not until after I'd assured her that I wasn't too broken up over what happened with Dan. I was upset, that much was true, but I could handle it. Besides, I wanted some time alone to think about the Ghost Guys, and come up with a plan of action.

A cursory internet search didn't turn up much on Mike Delacorte, or on any other members of his crew. The Ghost Guys website was basic and had lots of dark pictures of them skulking around cemeteries and abandoned buildings. The lack of decent photography, and the overall amateurish feel of their website, made me think they were a bunch of goofs. But, that didn't explain how these goofs had found me at the restaurant, or how they knew about me in the first place.

All of these loose ends were giving me a headache. I shut my laptop, kicked off my boots and laid on the couch. As soon as I did, someone knocked on my office door, but I ignored it. It was after hours, the door was locked, and I was beat. The problems of the world could wait for a while. Then, I got a text.

Dan: You at home? I'm at your door.
Eli: Yeah. One sec.

I dragged myself off the couch and opened the door. I was met by a very disheveled Dan Lyons bearing two cups of coffee.

"Hi," I said around a yawn. "What's up?"

"I just got off shift, and I wanted to see you." Confusion skated across his face, but it was gone in an instant. "I brought coffee."

"Thank the gods."

I took the proffered cup, and we went into the office's waiting room and sat on the couch.

"Why did you want to see me? Are you all right after yesterday?"

"I am, thanks to you. I still have no idea where that bullet ended up."

"Hopefully, it disintegrated inside the slug," I said. "Did you get in trouble for not going back to work yesterday?"

"I told them the restaurant gave us breakfast, and I spent the rest of the day sick as a dog," he replied. "After what we dug up on the cook, the chief thinks he spiked our food."

"What else happened with the cook?" I asked, hoping he hadn't been possessed again.

"That guy now has a litany of problems to deal with," Dan replied. "While his mind was trapped wherever he was, the creep using his body wandered all over town causing trouble. He's been caught on camera doing all sorts of shit."

"Anything bad?"

"Not really, but it does throw a wrench into his story about being kidnapped. Not that it was a story." Dan rubbed his eyes. "I believe this guy, one hundred percent, but I don't know if I can help him."

"I understand. When the supernatural world bleeds into the mortal one, people on both sides get hurt." When Dan remained silent, I asked, "Is that what you wanted to talk about?"

"No. Yes. I, ah, don't know." He drank some coffee. "I just felt like I needed to talk to you."

I looked at him for a long moment, then I dropped my gaze to my lap. "Do you remember anything from when you were possessed?"

"Nothing other than that hell room," he replied. "Why?" His eyes widened, and he added, "What did I do? Was it illegal?"

"It was not illegal." I balanced my elbows on my knees, held the coffee cup in my hands, and stared at the lid. "We had a moment."

"A moment? What the hell does that mean?" I met his gaze, and my expression must have told him all about what a moment is. "Holy shit. Are you okay?"

"Me? Yeah, I'm fine."

"Your tattoos didn't warn you that I was possessed?"

"No. Probably because the demon was in a human body. Your body." We sat in silence for a moment, then Dan laughed softly. "Are you going to tell me why you're laughing?"

"I've been trying to get you to go out with me for months. I get possessed, we have sex, and I don't even remember it."

"We did not have sex." I felt my face flush. "Not exactly."

He moved to touch my forearm, but halted halfway. "Is this okay?" he asked.

"What? Yeah. It's fine."

Dan touched my wrist. I shifted the coffee cup to my other hand and laced my fingers with his. "I suppose it's only fair to tell you what happened," I began, then I told him everything, from the shower, to the bedroom, up until when I realized that the demon was distracting me while it snooped around Dan's house. The story ended with me pouring a pound of salt down his throat. Unfortunately, that was the only part Dan remembered.

"I'm so sorry," I said after he'd heard everything. "I should have realized what was happening sooner. I should have known better, and gotten it out of you right away."

"Hey." Dan tilted my chin up with his thumb and forefinger. A hot tear rolled down my cheek and splashed onto his arm. "Hey. This is not your fault. You saved me, you know that, right?"

"But that creature used you," I said.

"It used you, too." Dan held out his arm, and I mashed myself against him. I couldn't stop the tears flowing down my cheeks. If he minded the waterworks, he kept it to himself. "Did I hurt you?"

"Dan, it wasn't you."

"It was my body," he said, his voice thick. "That makes it me. Goddamn it, Eli, if that thing used me to hurt you, I'll never forgive myself."

"It didn't hurt me. You did not hurt me."

"But, you said we—"

"I know." I deliberately did not look at him, and continued, "Everything I did, I did because I wanted to. It was consensual."

Dan settled back against the couch. Since his arm was wrapped around my shoulders, I went with him. "Oh." A pause. "I was not expecting you to say that."

"Well, I wasn't expecting any of it," I said. "But after you killed the slug adrenaline was high, we were in the shower together, and it just kind of happened. And it was you."

"Eli, you've repeatedly told me that we have a purely professional relationship."

"That's true, but I've always felt safe with you. That means a lot."

I'd expected a crass comeback, a double entendre so bad it could sour milk. Instead, Dan nestled me closer to him, then he kissed my hair. "You'll always be safe with me."

We sat together for a little while, both of us quiet as we finished our coffee. My mind was racing with what I'd told Dan, and how I was reacting to being close to him again. Even though I was dead certain that Dan hadn't been the one in control or even aware of his actions, after what had happened, I now felt more attracted to him than ever before. I wanted to snuggle with him on that couch all day, maybe take things further than we'd already gone.

And none of that could happen, because it was Dan. Not only did we work together, I'd basically told him a story about something he had no memory of. For all I knew, he thought I'd made the whole thing up as a way to get into his pants, or maybe as the world's worst come on. I could not expect Dan to reciprocate my strange and random desires. I didn't even know if these strange and random desires were the real thing, or if they were some kind of spell the demon had placed on me. Maybe I'd been spelled all along, and what Dan and I had done wasn't consensual.

I shuddered. Unless I learn beyond a shadow of a doubt that I was bespelled, I will never, ever share that idea with Dan. It would crush him.

"You cold?"

"What?" I asked, then I remembered that I'd shuddered. "No, I'm fine."

More silence. After a minute or so, Dan asked, "You said the demon was interested in something in my house?"

"It kept looking toward a certain spot in your yard, and another inside the house. It was staring at it as if there was something it needed." I looked at him for the first time since I'd told him what happened. Thankfully, he was the same old Dan. "Are you hiding demon artifacts in the walls?"

"Yeah, right next to my plaster cast of Bigfoot." He smirked. I giggled. Just like that, we were friends again. "Think we should check it out?"

The best part about Dan was that his mind worked like mine: when given a set of circumstances, he stacked up the clues and set about solving his case. "I'm free if you are."

CHAPTER 10

WHO'S CHARLOTTE?

D AN BLEW OUT A breath, and said, "Tell me how it happened."

"It all went down in less than a minute," I said. "It was crazy."

We were standing on Dan's front walkway, mere steps from where the demon slug had appeared right before Dan shot it. We'd searched the area, and there was no empty bullet casing, and no bullet holes in Dan's house, the surrounding trees, or his neighbor's house. Thank all the gods for that last bit.

"See that?" Dan pointed to a dull black lump set above and to the right of the front door. "That was a surveillance camera. Our monster destroyed it."

"Did the camera pick up anything?" I asked, not that I wanted to have a look at that slug ever again.

"Nope. It must have taken it out before we got here." Dan glanced around the front yard. "As far as the technology's concerned, it's like it never happened."

"What do you remember?" I asked.

"I remember reaching for the doorknob. Then you said something smart, and I looked back at you."

I remembered that moment too, since Dan had glanced at me over his shoulder wearing that sweet smile that erased his years of law enforcement and made him look like a fresh faced kid. God, Moore, get a grip.

"Do you remember seeing the demon?"

"I remember you looking up. The next thing I remember was being trapped in that dark room. The next time I was here, you were sitting on my chest choking me with salt."

I scuffed the sidewalk with the toe of my boot. "Salt was all I had to work with. That, and a few herbs."

He tilted up my chin. If he kept touching me, I was either going to punch him or kiss him. "You did great."

Maybe I'd punch him and then kiss him. "Seriously, you should consider keeping anti-possession supplies on hand. What if the salt and rosemary hadn't been enough?"

"All right. This weekend, you can take me shopping."

Ugh. I am just going to punch him and be done with it.

Dan unlocked his door, and we entered the house. To the left was the downstairs bedroom and adjacent bathroom. He started down the hall, and the jokes followed. "Here's where the kissing started?"

I glared at him. "There was no kissing."

Dan halted. "Really?"

"Yeah. It was one of the little things that made me realize it wasn't you."

Before he could respond, I breezed past him and entered his bedroom. "You were in here when the demon began staring at something."

"Staring at something in this room?"

"I'm not sure. You were about here," I said, standing next to the bed about where Dan had been when we'd, um, you know. "And staring out into the hallway."

"I was standing?"

I cleared my throat. "You were kneeling on the bed."

He hopped onto the bed and mimicked the position he'd been in. "Okay, Danny, what were you looking at?"

I realized he was facing the open door, and the hall beyond it. "Maybe you—it—was more interested in the hall." I moved to the doorway and examined the hallway. The wall opposite the door had a display of several-well composed scenery photographs. "What are these pictures of?"

Dan stood beside me. "Those are some of Charlotte's best work."

"Who's Charlotte?"

He rubbed the back of his neck. "I used to be married. Charlotte was my wife."

I swallowed hard. Just when I'd barely allowed myself to feel anything for him, I found out he had an ex-wife. "Oh. I didn't know that."

"Yeah, well, I don't really talk about her. She was sick, and the only thing that took her mind off her symptoms was her photography. Then she got sicker, and she could barely even do that."

His voice caught at the end, and I understood. Dan wasn't divorced. He was a widower. "Has it been a long time?" I asked.

"It'll be five years next July," he replied.

"I'm sorry."

"Yeah. Me, too." He took a breath, and just like that the grieving widower was replaced by Detective Daniel Lyons. This guy could compartmentalize like a champ. "The question now is why would some demon be interested in Charlotte's work?"

"It might not be the photography, so much as the places." I leaned forward and scrutinized an image of a sunset. "Do you know where these were taken?"

"Mostly in and around England," he replied. "She was what you'd call an Anglophile, and a trip to England had been on Charlotte's bucket list for years. She spent a few summers there as a kid, and always wanted to go back. She saved for years, then we won a lottery and got the trip for our honeymoon."

"Wait. You and Charlotte won a trip to England, she took lots of pictures, and now you get possessed and the demon possessing you is interested in those same pictures? Dan, this is not a coincidence."

"Same question. Why would a demon be interested in Charlotte's photography?" he asked.

"I don't know the answer to that. But what I do know is that this," I tapped one of the framed photographs, "is the entrance to one of the world's most famous poison gardens."

I carefully took down all of Charlotte's photographs while Dan hauled boxes of albums up from the basement. I couldn't imagine what he was going through emotionally. He'd obviously loved his wife a great deal, and bringing up so much of the past all at once could not be easy for him. I mean, I was totally freaking out just because he'd been married. He must be on track for a full on breakdown.

I set the framed photographs on the coffee table, and Dan unpacked the boxes and organized the albums into neat stacks. There were dozens of albums.

"Charlotte was certainly prolific," I said, surveying the heaps of pages we needed to go through.

"She loved her camera," Dan said. "She always said that when she was looking through the lens it didn't matter how she felt, or what the side effects from her meds were. She said that the camera was the great equalizer, and with it she made her own story."

"I'm sorry," I said, then I bit my lip. "I should stop saying that. People have been telling me that they're sorry for my entire life, and I know how annoying it gets."

Dan looked at me and cocked his head. "Why are people apologizing to you?"

"For my mother taking off, my dad not being around much, Gran's death," I rattled off. "I'm quite the sob story."

"Your mom took off?"

"Yeah. The first time my seer abilities manifested she freaked out and had me put in a psych ward," I replied.

"Shit. How old were you?"

"I was in the third grade." I picked up the photograph of the poison garden's gate. "You know, that incident was when Sarah Allwood first possessed Jada."

"Huh." Dan looked over the many albums and boxes of photographs. "If we're going to do this, we'll need fuel."

"I'll make some coffee." I went into his kitchen and went to work on the coffee maker. "Are you hungry? We can make snacks, too."

When he didn't answer, I turned around and saw him staring at me. "What?"

"How do you know where everything is?" he asked.

"Oh." I set down the coffee grounds. "While you were possessed, I told the demon I was going to make something to eat, then I went through all the cabinets looking for supplies. I was killing time hoping the demon didn't know I was on to it while I tried to figure out how to get it out of you."

He looked rattled, and I couldn't say I blamed him. When he spoke, he surprised me. "Is that why I'm out of eggs?"

"Hey, I didn't have a lot to work with." I turned back to the coffeemaker. "I'm just glad you grow your own herbs. I don't know if that would have worked without the rosemary."

"I'm just glad you were here with me."

The weight of his words unnerved me. I shook it off and finished setting up the coffee maker. When I turned around I saw Dan hunting through the fridge.

"There's nothing here worth eating. We're gonna have to order in," he declared as he shut the freezer. "Pizza?"

"Pizza sounds great."

Dan ordered while I washed two coffee mugs. Once the coffee was brewed we took our mugs and returned to the living room. We sat on the couch, and Dan looked over the framed photographs.

"You really think there's a clue in here?" he asked.

"There must be," I replied. "That demon targeted you for a reason, and it wouldn't stop staring at these photographs. They're all from England?"

"The ones on that wall are, yeah."

I did not comment on how he kept a visual reminder of his deceased wife across from his bedroom. As tributes went, it was rather sweet. "Why was Charlotte so interested in England?"

"She loved everything British," he replied. "British music, television, you name it. If it was British, she was into it."

"Was her family from there?"

"No. She was French."

I filed that fact away, and picked up an album. The pages were filled with photographs taken in a well-tended garden. "Was she interested in gardening?"

"She sure was," he replied. "She kept a garden, until it was too much for her."

"Was the garden here?"

"Yeah."

"Can I see it?"

He shrugged. "Sure, but there isn't much left of it."

He led me out the back door and into the yard. He had a huge yard, perfect for growing herbs and vegetables. There was even a small greenhouse off to the side.

"She wasn't much interested in vegetables," he said, nodding toward the raised beds near the greenhouse. "She grew fancy flowers, exotic plants and weird herbs, things like that. Stuff you'd be into," he added.

"Nice." I approached the older flower beds. It was apparent that nothing new had been planted for some time, but Dan had kept up with the weeding. Apparently, Charlotte had gravitated toward perennials, because some of the plants were still identifiable.

I extended my arm across Dan's body, barring his way. "Don't go any closer."

"Why not?"

"Everything in this bed is poisonous."

The back corner of the raised bed was dominated by a huge white snakeroot plant, which was so toxic that if you ate the beef of a cow that had eaten said snakeroot, you'd still die. There were also groupings of aconite, hemlock, and my favorite poison, belladonna.

"Are you sure?"

"Positive." I looked at the greenhouse. "What do you grow in there?"

"Nothing. It's all leftovers from Charlotte."

I nodded, then I entered the greenhouse. It was pretty dilapidated, and mostly held dusty old pots and some gardening tools. It also had a huge potted castor oil plant.

"So that plant is where ricin comes from," I said, and Dan's eyes widened. I faced him. "This is all a little weird."

"More than a little," Dan said, then he glanced at his watch. "I'm gonna pick up the pizza."

He went to get our food, and I returned to the living room. I peeked inside one of the boxes from the basement and saw something white and frilly. It was Dan and Charlotte's wedding album.

Curiosity overtook me, and I opened the album. The first picture was of Dan and Charlotte dressed in their wedding clothes, and standing under a floral arch. Dan was wearing a tuxedo with a white tie and vest. He looked happier than I've ever seen him. And as for Charlotte, well, she was gorgeous.

She had dark hair curled into neat tendrils that grazed her shoulders. Her skin was pale, and she had rosy cheeks, and big, bright eyes. She was thin, bordering on skinny, and I wondered if that was due to her sickness. Her overall appearance reminded me of a Victorian woman stricken with tuberculosis; they'd been considered ideal beauties with their bright eyes and reddened cheeks and lips, all of it due to symptoms from the disease making them attractive. Beauty standards were weird.

I flipped through the album and saw page after page of Dan and Charlotte gazing lovingly at each other, dancing together, feeding each other cake. Throughout it all, I noticed a few things: Charlotte wasn't just thin, she was emaciated, and everyone in the frame with her looked as if they were keeping an eye out in case she stumbled. What the hell had this woman been sick with?

My fingers started to tingle, then the sensation slowly spread up my forearms. Something had triggered my foresight. The feeling was familiar enough, yet I'd never come to enjoy it. Unlike speaking to the dead, my foresight wasn't a straightforward ability. It was fickle, and cranky, and had never once helped me or anyone else. But, now that the feeling had begun, there was nothing else to do but see what it decided to show me.

Maybe this time, it will be helpful. I closed my eyes, and saw a car accident. The car was on its roof, and I couldn't tell what make or model it was. I looked away from the wrecked vehicle and saw a group of six people standing in a field. Two of the people seemed familiar, but at that distance I couldn't recognize them any more than the car. The other four individuals, though, they were definitely witches, and very, very powerful ones.

"Honey, I'm home," Dan announced as he entered carrying a pizza box and a bag of extras. I blinked myself out of the vision and made a mental note to make sure my car insurance was in order. I also needed to figure out why I was going to be at a meeting of at least four powerful witches.

"I'm in here," I called. Dan entered the room, and stopped short when he saw the photo album in my lap.

"I hope you don't mind," I said. I decided then and there not to mention my vision, at least not until I understood what was happening in it. The poor guy just got over a possession, and he did not need more things to worry about. "I wasn't trying to be nosy. I was curious."

He smiled. "Occupational hazard, huh? I got that too. Come on, let's get some plates."

I followed him into the kitchen and helped him unpack the food. He'd gotten a spinach salad to go with the pizza.

"What'd you think of the pictures?" he asked.

"I think Charlotte was beautiful, and that you two looked like you were very happy together."

"We were happy. Even though she's gone, I know how lucky I am to have had the time I did with her."

I turned away, and added, "You look nice in a tux, too."

Dan leaned close, and said, "I've still got it. Maybe later I'll put it on for you."

I burst out laughing, mostly because his warm breath on my neck was driving me crazy, partly because I'd slipped again. I'd flirted with Dan before, but never this blatantly, and now I couldn't stop. If I couldn't get a handle on my emotions, he'd think I was into him.

I was starting to wonder if I really was attracted to him, or if I was just feeling the leftovers from what had happened during his possession.

I served the salad, then I grabbed a slice of pizza. "Pepperoni and mushroom, my favorite."

"Is it?" Dan reached into his refrigerator and pulled out two beers. "Beer?"

"Why not?"

He opened the beers and set one in front of me. We ate in silence for a few moments. "This turned out to be a strange day," he said at length.

"It sure has." I glanced at the clock. "When's your next shift?"

"Tomorrow," he replied. "Hopefully, we can make some headway on our latest demon before I have to go in."

"Hopefully." I drank some beer, hoping the alcohol could muddle my foresight enough to keep it quiet for the rest of the night. "Is it okay if I ask you about Charlotte?"

"Questions are free," he replied. "If you go too far, I'll tell you."

"You said she was sick," I began. "What did she have?"

"Here's the thing. No one really knew," he replied. "They did dozens of tests on her, but every one of them turned up negative. Most though she was a hypochondriac, but her symptoms were the real deal."

"Her symptoms didn't point to a particular disease?"

"They were present, but vague. She had a hard time eating because of severe nausea. As a result of the lack of eating, she was weak. She had trouble breathing, and this cough that would come and go. Sometimes she'd cough so hard she'd hack up blood."

"That does not sound vague," I said.

"I hear ya, and I yelled at every doctor on the east coast about it," he said. "But no matter how Char suffered, whatever symptoms she had didn't point to anything specific. We spent years treating symptoms, not curing whatever caused them. And then, one day..." He shook his head.

"I know it's stupid to replay past mistakes over and over again, but I can't help feeling like I could have done something more for her. Should have. But we followed the doctor's orders, I made sure she took her meds and got her exercise, and she died anyway."

I reached across the table and squeezed his hand. "You did everything you could."

"How do you know? You weren't even there."

"I know you."

We stared at each other, the air heavy around us. His fingers tightened on mine, and I had a flashback of those fingers rinsing my hair in the shower. "I-I can't eat anymore right now." I got up and put my still-full plate in the fridge. "Do you have something I can make notes with?"

"Sure do," Dan replied, and soon enough we were back on the couch, flipping through photo albums and taking notes. I started by categorizing the photographs, and made lists cross referencing locations and times. Thankfully, there were precious few pictures of Charlotte and Dan together outside of the wedding album.

"She hated having her picture taken," Dan said. "Thought she was too pale, too skinny, too whatever. Always said she was more comfortable behind the camera."

"She was in her element." I flipped a page, and was confronted by a picture of a dilapidated Victorian greenhouse. It was a dead ringer for the one Bennet had shipped over from England and installed at the college.

"Dan, do you remember when this was taken?"

He leaned over and peered at the picture. "That's from where she used to spend summers as a kid. I never went there."

"Huh." I leaned back, and considered that Bennet's purchasing of the greenhouse had been aided by Nathaniel Beauclaire, then masquerading as Nicholas Atwood. Nathaniel had wanted that greenhouse here. I thought about Charlotte's symptoms, which while debilitating didn't point to any specific disease.

Shit. Dan's wife had been possessed, and the entity had eventually killed her.

"Dan," I began, then I glanced to the side. His head was tilted back in sleep, beer bottle precariously balanced on his leg. I remembered that he'd come by my place right after work; poor guy had to be exhausted. I took the bottle and set it on the coffee table, then I went back to my research. I needed to know who—or what—had possessed Charlotte.

I blinked myself awake, momentarily not knowing where I was. It all came rushing back to me: the photographs, the pizza, Dan. And Dan's wife, Charlotte. I'd been searching through her old photo albums for clues. I remembered setting down my notes, and stretching. I moved to stretch again, and realized I was laying on top of Dan.

Sometime during our nap we'd ended up lying on the length of the couch, and the blanket that had been tossed across the back was now tucked around us. I wondered if Dan had done that. What I did know was that I was warm, he smelled amazing, and that I did not want to stop snuggling just yet. Being so close to him was like heaven. Since he was still asleep I laid my head on his chest, my hand over his heart. He shifted, and one of his hands landed square on my butt.

Not like his hands haven't been to more interesting places. Since he'd started feeling me up first, I slid my hand underneath his shirt and sunk my fingers into the soft curls on his pecs. Then he squeezed my butt, and I yelped.

"I thought you were sleeping," I said.

"I was, until you started pulling on my chest hair."

I tugged hard on his hair. He laughed, and squeezed my butt again. "I guess we're even now."

"Yeah." He moved his hand up to my back, but other than that made no move to get up. I kept my hand right where it was, like each of us was daring the other to move first.

"I'm sorry you got blindsided about Charlotte," he said. "If we'd ever dated or anything I would have told you. Hell, I've almost told you about her a bunch of times, but I didn't want you to think I was pulling a grieving widower act on you."

"Guys do that? Just to get girls to date them?" I placed my hands one on top of the other on his chest, and balanced my chin on top of them. "I'm shocked."

He smirked. "I bet you are." His joking demeanor gone, he tucked a piece of hair behind my ear. "The truth is that while I'll always love Char, I know she's gone. I miss her, but I'm not going to live my life pining for her."

"That's probably the best way to honor her memory."

His thumb caressed my cheek. "You think?"

"She loved you. She'd want you to be happy."

His fingers moved to my neck, then they sunk into my hair. "I'm pretty happy right now."

"Yeah?"

"Yeah."

Dan's hands grasped my waist, then he hauled me up his body and kissed me. It was a sweet, soft kiss, and he made no demands to take things further. When we parted I settled against him, my cheek pressed against his throat.

"I probably should have asked first, but you have seen me naked," he said, and I laughed. "I needed to even the playing field."

"It's gonna take more than a kiss, buddy."

"I'm just getting started."

CHAPTER 11

PLANT DUTY (AND CAT DUTY)

"YOU SHOULD PROBABLY GET some real sleep," I said, since he'd worked the whole day after being possessed, and had spent the next few hours wrapped up in our latest demon mystery. We were still laying on the couch, snuggling and making small talk. There hadn't been any more kissing, which was unfortunate. Dan was a pretty good kisser.

"You're probably right. I'll take you home."

We moved to sit upright. Both of us were a little clumsy, bumping into each other as if neither of us wanted to break contact just yet. He walked me to the door, and I remembered why I'd come to his house in the first place.

"You never showed me the information you found about Jada, and the halfway house she's going to."

"Shit, I forgot all about that. Does that mean you'll come over again tomorrow?"

I paused, my mouth open like a fish out of water. "I-I guess."

His head drooped. "I'm sorry. I bet you can hardly stand to look at me after what happened."

I stepped closer to him and ducked my head so I could see his eyes. "If you thought I couldn't stand to look at you, why did you kiss me on the couch?"

He rested his forehead against mine. "Thought it might be my last chance."

I stood on my toes and pecked his cheek. "Wasn't."

"Eli. Eliza." Dan's hand cupped the back of my head, while the other one snaked around my waist. "You know how I always say what I mean, right?"

"I do." It was one of the aspects I most appreciated about him.

"Okay. So. I am so fricken' conflicted right now I don't know which way is up. The possession, dragging out all Char's stuff and reliving that, and now this whole new mystery. But I am certain about one thing."

"What's that?"

He placed his hand against my cheek. "I really wish you were coming to bed with me."

I inhaled sharply. "Straight talk, right?"

He nodded. "Always."

"I'm confused, too. I think I need some time, if that's okay." I turned into his palm, loving the feel of his hand against my cheek. "Want to try and figure all of this out together?"

Dan grinned, and my heart did a little somersault. "I'd love to."

The ride back to my place took about ten minutes, which was preferable to the hour-long walk I'd have otherwise. When we got to my building, Dan shut the car off, took off his seat belt, and faced me.

"What?" I asked, since he obviously wanted to say something.

"I don't know if I should keep telling you what's on my mind," he replied. "I don't want to lay it on too thick."

"If it's what you feel, then it isn't wrong." When he dropped his gaze, I said, "Tessa and I have an agreement that when we're holding hands we can tell each other anything, no matter how wild or embarrassing. It's our safety zone."

"You and Tess hold hands a lot?"

"Whenever we need to." I put my hand on top of his. "So, talk to me."

He smiled at our hands. "I've brought you home so many times, and I never once got to kiss you goodnight."

"Well, you never asked."

"You're right. I never did." Dan pressed the release button on my seat belt, then he leaned across the center console and touched my cheek. "Can I?"

"Can you what?"

"Kiss you, dammit!"

"Not if I kiss you first." I leaned over and pressed my lips to his, which surprised him; I wondered if he'd thought I'd just been humoring his attraction for me, and hadn't realized I was attracted to him too. Well, that cat was out of the bag.

Dan slid his hand from my cheek down my neck, coming to rest on the small of my back. When I would have moved away, his arms went rigid, then his tongue stroked my lips. My mouth parted under his as I wound my arms around his neck, and let him devour me.

When we parted, he held me close for a moment. My knees were weak and my heart was pounding as if I'd run a marathon. If he'd asked me right then to go to bed with him, I don't know if I'd have been able to decline. But he didn't ask, so I got to pretend I could resist him for a little bit longer.

"Well, um, good night," I said.

"I'll call you in the morning," he said.

"You know where to find me."

Dan leaned across the car and opened the door for me, and watched me as I walked toward my building and opened the door. I missed him already.

Once I was inside my apartment, the first thing I did was shower. Something about the hot water rinsing over my head had always helped me clear the cobwebs out of my mind.

After I'd toweled off, I settled at my desk and started listing everything I knew about Nathaniel Beauclaire. It seemed that he had a legion of lesser demons working for him, which was both unusual and terrifying. One clue I needed more information on was Bennet's greenhouse. If that really was the same greenhouse Charlotte had photographed when she was a child, that put a whole new spin on this case. What kind of spin, now that was the question.

I picked up my phone to call Bennet, and saw the time. It was after midnight, and while I knew Bennet was a night owl it was too late to call anyone, never mind the mild mannered local shepherd. I closed my laptop, grabbed my phone and my charger cord, and went to bed.

It felt like my head had only just hit the pillow when a call vibrated me awake. I felt around for my phone, then my bleary eyes stared at the screen. It was Dan, calling me when he woke up just like he'd promised. I got the feeling that Dan kept a lot of promises.

"Hey," I said.

"Hey, yourself. What are you doing?"

"Literally nothing. The phone woke me up."

"Oh, I'm sorry."

"It's okay." A small eternity of silence passed between us. "Aren't you working today?"

"I called in a sick day. I'm off until next week."

"Oh. Nice."

More silence, which was somehow louder than either of our voices. Eventually, Dan spoke. "Can I ask you something?"

"Yeah. Ask me anything."

"What are we?"

"Um, people?"

"I mean, to each other." When I didn't respond, he continued, "There was everything that happened while I was possessed, and while I don't remember any of that we did have a pretty intense goodbye last night."

I opened my mouth to talk, but he kept going, "And I know you said you need time, and I get it. I do. I will give you all the time you need, Eli, I swear I will, but I'm laying here in bed on the phone and I haven't done that since high school. I thought of you the second I woke up, couldn't even do anything until I heard your voice. Does that... Does that mean anything to you?"

"It does. It means a lot." I pictured Dan in bed, all alone in his big house. "Are you lonely? I mean, you have that house all to yourself."

"I wouldn't say I'm lonely, but the house is too much for one person. I can't even keep up with the yard on my own, so I have a landscaping company handle it. Maybe I should warn them about the poisonous plants out back."

I laughed. "Probably a good idea, unless you want a couple zombie gardeners hanging around."

"Could be good for Halloween." He paused. "I had a lot of plans for the future, which was how I ended up with this place. For a while I thought about selling, but I like it here."

"It is a nice house. At least, the parts I saw were nice."

"Tell you what, next time you're here I'll give you the grand tour."

"I like tours." I burrowed under the blankets, remembering how Dan and I had cuddled on his couch. "I'm glad you're not lonely."

"Me, too. So, what are you up to today?"

"Let me check my planner." I got out of bed and padded into my office. "Oh, I have to go to Gran's and water the plants." I remembered how much I'd wanted to see Dan's house, and asked, "Want to come with me?"

"I'd love to," he said; I swear I could hear the smile in his voice. "I'll pick you up in an hour."

It didn't take me long to get ready. Since I had some time to kill while I waited for Dan, I called Bennet and asked him about the greenhouse.

"How did you even find out about it?" I asked.

"I'd just been granted the funds to purchase a new greenhouse for the school," he replied. "Then the problem became that I could not find new construction that was adequate for our needs. I started looking into salvage companies, and that's how I located the English one. I must say, it was in much better condition than any of the newer ones."

"Yes, it was beautiful," I said. "So this salvaged greenhouse was cheaper than a new one, even though it was shipped over from England?"

"I found that odd myself," Bennet replied. "However, since we already had the foundations *in situ* I was only paying for the glass framework. The company even threw in a few Victorian era pots."

"Huh."

"Eli, why the sudden interest in the greenhouse's provenance?"

"Dan's wife used to spend her summers at an English estate, and took pictures of a greenhouse that looked a lot like yours. I'm wondering if they're the same."

"Dan has a wife?"

"Had. She died."

"Oh, that's very sad. I must remember to offer my condolences." I heard a pen scratching against paper. "Have you thought to ask Tessa about this development?"

"That's a good idea. I'll ask her when I see her."

"I'll do some research on the location the greenhouse came from. I'll contact you once I have something."

"Sounds like a plan."

Bennet and I said our goodbyes. I sat at my desk for a while, staring off into space and thinking about the past few days. I still had no idea what to do about Nathaniel Beauclaire, this latest demon, Charlotte's photographs, or Dan.

Dan: Do you want me to bring you anything?

Eli: I'm good.

Dan: Coffee? Bagel?

Eli: Stop trying to buy me things and just get here.

Dan: Yes, ma'am.

I set down my phone and sipped my home brewed coffee, and thought about that text exchange. Why was Dan so intent on bringing me something? He knew I was home, with everything I needed right here at my fingertips. What's more, we were going to Gran's house, a short drive across town. While I appreciate offerings of coffee as much as the next person, he needed to take it down a notch.

I heard a knock at the door; there was the coffee courier now. I opened the door, and presented him with a travel mug of his very own filled with coffee. "Only sugar, just how you like it."

"Thanks." He moved toward me, and abruptly halted.

"What's wrong?" I demanded, momentarily terrified he was possessed again.

"I was going to kiss you, but I don't know if we're kiss hello-type people." He frowned. "Are we?"

"I don't think I've ever kissed anyone hello." I bit my lip; the next thing I said would set the tone for whatever was growing between us. "But you have?"

"No, not really." Dan brought my hand to his mouth and kissed my knuckles. "But you're not like anyone I've ever known, and I want to do things differently."

My breath caught in my throat, my fingers hot where Dan gripped them. I wanted to pull him inside and shut the door, and spend the day figuring out whatever this was. But, the plants needed watering, and I needed to get my head on straight.

I squeezed his fingers, then I grabbed my own travel mug along with my bag and keys. "I'm ready if you are."

"Always." He stepped back into the hall while I closed and locked the door. "What's this house's address?"

"Thirty-one Essex Street. It's right past—"

"I know where Essex Street is. It's near your buddy Jacob's house." We started down the stairs, and a minute or so later we were in Dan's shiny black SUV.

"When the town was settled back in the day, the witch families congregated on and around the hill, and the mortals chose the flatter areas. I always assumed it was because the flat areas were better for farmland."

"Witches didn't have farms?"

"They may have owned them, but they certainly didn't work them. Anyway, the seers ended up settling between the witches and the mortals, because that's what we are. The line between the magical and the mundane."

Dan glanced at me. "There's nothing mundane about you, babe."

I didn't know what to say to that, but I did know that was at least the third time Dan had called me babe. "How old are you?"

"Thirty-five."

"I thought you were older," I muttered. "How old were you when you got married?"

"Twenty-two. I got my driver's license at seventeen, graduated high school at eighteen, and entered the police academy at twenty-four."

I slid down in my seat. "I wasn't trying to be nosy, but you're acting like we have this burgeoning romance and I feel like I need to know things about you."

"That's fair. How old are you?"

"Twenty-eight. I'll be twenty-nine next month."

"Think I'm too old for you?"

"Do you?" Before I could answer, Dan turned onto Essex Street. "It's the blue house with the old iron fence."

We rounded the curve, and Dan leaned over the steering wheel as he stared at up Gran's house. "You grew up here? In a mansion?"

"It's not a mansion. It just has a lot of rooms. The driveway's there."

I indicated the gravel driveway. Dan pulled off the street, and followed the driveway to the old carriage house. Gran had converted it into a garage in the fifties. Beyond the carriage house were the badly-tended gardens that someone, probably me, should take a look at before the became a full on jungle. The house towered over the yard, four stories of intricate wood trim and ancient leaded glass windows. It was definitely the showstopper of the neighborhood, which was just how Gran had liked it.

I unlocked the back door and stepped inside. It wasn't too stuffy, but I started opening windows in the mudroom for some fresh air, anyway. I'd just opened the third window when I heard the stampede.

"Here they come," I said.

"Here who come?" Dan asked, then the Feline Federation bounded into the mudroom to say hello. I crouched down to say hello and bestow the mandatory scritches.

"Let me introduce you to Smokey, Pumpkin, and Muffuletta," I said, introducing the gray, calico and tabby in turn. "They're super friendly."

"You leave three cats locked up by themselves in this house?" Dan demanded. "All alone?" Well, now I knew he was an animal lover.

"Dan." I stood, Pumpkin in my arms. "They're ghosts. Remember, I told you about them?"

He stared at me, then Pumpkin. "Yeah. I didn't expect them to be so... alive."

"They were Gran's cats when she was a kid. When they died she brought their spirits back, but she gave them a little extra oomph. It's why they feel solid, like real cats." I thrust Pumpkin into Dan's arms. He petted her, and she purred. "No one knows how Gran managed to make them so lifelike. We thought they'd fade after she passed, but here we are."

"Here we are, indeed." Dan set Pumpkin on her feet, and watched her romp with the other two. "It's like how you made Jacob Allwood almost alive again."

"I wouldn't say he's almost alive."

"No one would believe he's dead." Dan was right; almost no one thought Jacob was dead, not even the people who'd found his body.

"I leave that sort of big thinking to Bennet. Come on. Watering cans won't fill themselves."

I led Dan out of the mudroom and through the back parlor. To the left of the parlor was the main staircase, and the dining room was on the right. "Why don't you live here?" Dan asked.

"Too many memories."

"Then why not sell?"

"Same reason. Too many memories." I went into the kitchen and started filling watering cans. "Technically, my father inherited the house. When he's in the area he stays here. The rest of the time, I'm on plant duty."

"And cat duty."

I handed him a watering can. "Don't let them hear you. If they decide you like them, they'll be all over you."

"That's cool. I like cats."

Of course he did, because with every word and deed Dan was proving he was ideal relationship material. So why was I so hesitant to pursue anything with him?

Because my last relationship had been a train wreck, that's why.

"This way," I said once the watering cans were full, and I led him through the sitting room and to a set of glass paneled doors. I opened them, and said, "This is Gran's solarium. It's original to the house. She turned it into her very own poison garden."

"Wow." Dan stepped inside the glass-paneled room, awe surrounding him like a cloak, and well it should. The solarium was octagonal, with a high arched roof and delicate iron filigree details. Plants hung from the ceiling and were lined up in pots, and the furniture and bookcases were all antique white, which softened the look of the dark slate floor.

"This is my favorite room," I said, bending to water the white oleander. "I used to read in here for hours, pretending I was in another world."

"This is another world," Dan said. "Think this is the look Bennet was going for with his greenhouse?"

"Maybe. It would explain why he bothered shipping one across the Atlantic." I stood, and lifted the watering can to one of the hanging plants. "He always liked Gran's solarium, too."

"He must have been like a kid in a candy store in here. Hey!"

Dan bumped into my back, and I lost my grip on the watering can as the contents spilled across the front of my shirt. "What happened?"

"The cats, I forgot about them." I turned around and saw Pumpkin siting on the floor, cleaning her paw. Dan looked at me, his mouth open as if to apologize, then his gaze dipped lower and he turned away. I looked down; my white shirt was soaked, and close to transparent.

"I'm sorry," he said.

"It's fine," I began, and almost made a comment about how he'd seen it all before. Only, he didn't remember any of that. "I've got clothes in my old room. I'll be right back."

I turned toward the staircase before he had a chance to say anything else, and did my best not to stomp up the steps like a petulant teenager. Although annoying, it had been an accident. I was certain Dan hadn't meant to bump into me, and even more certain he wasn't trying to set up an impromptu wet tee shirt contest. If anything Pumpkin had been playing matchmaker; she was the sneakiest member of the Feline Federation.

Once I was in my old room I flung open the wardrobe, and was confronted with the myriad black clothes that marked my Goth phase. So much for avoiding petulant teenager me. My clothing's color palette hadn't really evolved, but these days I tended to wear jeans instead of ripped tights.

I peeled off my soaked tee shirt and bra and set them on top of the hamper, then I pulled on a black tank top and a blue plaid shirt. I grabbed my wet clothes, stopped in the master bathroom and tossed them over the shower curtain rod to dry, and went back downstairs. Dan was waiting for me at the bottom of the steps.

"I know you don't want to hear the s-word," he began, "but maybe I can make it up to you another way." He pressed a button on his phone, and Big Band music flowed into the room.

"You keep these old timey songs queued up on your phone?"

"What can I say. I have an app." He bowed and extended his hand, and I realized he wanted to dance.

"Well, okay." I took his hand and Dan pulled me close. After a bit of fumbling we had our hands in the proper positions, and were swaying to the music.

"This is nice," he said.

"It is." Dan nestled me closer, and I laid my cheek against his chest. It was as perfect a moment as I'd ever had, romantic or otherwise, and for a split second I imagined being with Dan, and having a life with him that was all about making breakfast together in the morning, and slow dancing in the kitchen at night.

The second passed, and all of my doubts crept up to the surface.

"I don't want to be your rebound woman," I said into his chest.

"I don't feel like I'm rebounding."

"What does it feel like?"

"Like I'm moving on. Moving on to something…" He shook his head. "I was going to say better, but that's not the right word."

"Something worse?" I offered.

He tilted up my chin. "Something that feels right."

Dan held me with a gaze so strong even my urge to flee couldn't make me move. And why did I want to flee? Rationally, I understood that the only reason we were here was because of his possession. If that demon hadn't forced the two of us together I'd still be sidestepping Dan's advances and pretending I felt nothing for him. But what if that wasn't the only reason we were here, now? What if we would have eventually ended up together, demon or not?

I cleared my throat. "There's a lot you don't know about me."

"There's a lot you don't know about me, too." Dan slid his hand around to the back of my head and cradled me against him, then we resumed dancing. I liked dancing with him. "I wasn't always a cop, you know."

"Let me guess, you were the high school's star quarterback?"

He laughed, a deep rumble in his chest. "Not hardly. I was way too much of a troublemaker."

"Oh, so you were a stoner?"

"I never mentioned drug use. Why, Miss Moore? Is there something you'd like to confess?"

I hid my face against his chest so he wouldn't see me smile. "I plead the fifth."

Chapter 12

Something Of A Legend

When the first song ended, I didn't pull away. Neither did Dan, and we danced through three more numbers before I asked, "How many songs are there?"

He shrugged. "A lot. Do you want to stop?"

"The plants. I only watered one of them."

"How often do you come by?"

"Two, sometimes three times a week."

"That's a lot of watering. Can I dip you?"

"Um, okay." Dan dipped me, which was as exhilarating as going down the first drop on a roller coaster. Then he pulled me upright, and the second part of the dip was just as much of a rush as the first. "That was fun," I said, around my laughter.

"It was. Ever take one of those ballroom dance classes?"

"No. Have you?"

"Obviously not. Maybe we should do something like that. A couple thing."

I linked my hands behind his neck. "There you go, trying to make us a couple again."

"You found me out. You're a great detective."

"Am I?"

"You're perfect," he said, then he lowered his head and kissed me. I don't know if all the blood had rushed to my head when he dipped me or what, but it was the best kiss I'd ever had; better than when we'd said goodbye last night, better than when we kissed outside the Allwood Compound.

We stopped moving, and Dan deepened the kiss. One of his hands tangled in my hair while the other flattened against my lower back, pressing me against him. I'd just pulled him closer when Dan went still as a statue.

"Back door," he whispered. Dan killed the music, and I heard the door click shut. "Who else comes over here?"

"No one," I said, then I heard footsteps and the cats running toward the door. They only did that for me and one other living person, but I could hardly believe he was here.

"Dad?" I called.

"Eli?" Dad exited the mudroom with Muffuletta and Smokey in his arms, and Pumpkin draped across his shoulders. "I didn't know you'd be here."

I crossed the room and hugged him around the cats. I hadn't seen my father in person since a few days after Gran's memorial, and I'd missed him terribly. I'd long ago gotten used to him being gone for months at a time, but I'd never grown to like it. "I'm here to water the plants. I didn't know you were coming home. Are you here to become the Master Seer?"

"No, Bug. That's your calling." Dad kissed the top of my head. "I had some time, and I thought I'd come see what you were up to. Who's this?"

I stepped back and said, "Dad, this is Dan Lyons. Dan, this is my father, Alexander Moore."

"A pleasure, sir," Dan extended his hand, and he and Dad shook. "You're something of a legend around here."

"Am I?" Dad tilted his head to the side. "I hope I'm the good sort of legend. Is Tessa here, too?"

"No, just me and Dan." Dad raised an eyebrow, which I ignored. "Are you hungry? There's not really any food here, except plant food, but I can make us lunch at my place."

"Or we could go out for lunch," Dan said. "My treat."

"That's very generous of you, but I've been traveling for almost a week straight," Dad replied. "If it's all right with you, I was planning on resting for the rest of the day. Can we wait until tomorrow to catch up?"

"We can," I said, then I hugged him again. "I missed you."

"Missed you, too, Bug." Dad straightened, and added, "It was nice to meet you, Dan."

"You as well, Mr. Moore."

Dad laughed softly. "My friends call me Alex. I realize we've just met, but if you're friends with Eli, that's all the information I need."

Dan and I left so my father could get some rest, or as much rest as the Feline Federation would allow him to have. The cats adored Dad, and whenever he came home, they spent every waking moment terrorizing him. Good thing cats slept a lot, even ghost cats.

We got into the car, and Dan backed down the driveway. "Your father seems cool."

"He is. I wish he was home more, but his work takes him all over the world."

"He's a seer, like you?"

"Not exactly. He can speak to and summon the dead, and help spirits cross over, but he deals more in the magical side of things."

Dan paused to glance at me, then he put the car in drive and headed down the street. "Talking to dead people isn't magical?"

"That's just part of life. Dad manipulates the forces of life and death to keep seers safe, and help us do our work." I pushed up my shirt sleeve, revealing my seer's mark. "It's what he does as a marksman."

"He imbues these forces into the tattoo ink, which in turn keeps you safe," Dan concluded. "But that's not all he does?"

"No. He travels to various covens, renewing treaties between witches and seers, and making sure some portals remain open."

"Why only some? To keep too many people from dying at once?"

"No. We can't control who lives and who dies." I pulled down my sleeve, suddenly chilled. "Some of the portals are dangerous, so we keep people away from them."

"He does all of this by himself?"

I nodded. "Dad is the only living marksman."

"Sounds like he could use an assistant."

I remembered the endless stretches of time when Dad was gone while I was growing up, how much I needed him, but I hadn't wanted to reach out and distract him from his work. Then I was kidnapped and held in that basement for weeks, and Dad not only dropped everything to come home and rescue me, the next time he left, he took me on the road with him. I'd loved traveling with my father, seeing new places and learning not only about what he did, but about all the other people and cultures he worked with.

Then we went to Iran—which Dad still called Persia—and that was where I met Amir. I'd just turned eighteen, and Amir had seemed exotic and brilliant and so, so handsome. We'd kept in touch, and when Tessa and I went to Paris for my twenty-fourth birthday, Amir brought me a present. That had led to a two-year relationship that had turned me inside out and proved that everything I'd ever suspected about love was true: it didn't exist.

The worst part was that whenever I thought of Amir, my heart ached for him, even all these years later.

"Hey." Dan reached over and took my hand. "You got quiet."

"Sorry. I was thinking."

"About?"

"You don't want to know."

"Try me." When I remained silent, he added, "Straight talk, remember?"

I took a deep breath; he'd asked for it. "I was thinking about my ex."

"Oh." Dan's face and voice were expressionless, a massive feat of control for someone who wore his heart on his sleeve. "He live around here?"

"As far as I know, he's still in Paris."

Dan visibly deflated. "Good. I don't like competition."

"Believe me, he is not competition." I sat up straighter and shoved my memories of Amir as far away as they would go. "Do you have that information on Jada?"

Dan jerked his head toward the back seat. "It's in the back. Manila folder in my briefcase."

I let go of Dan's hand, unfastened my seatbelt, and turned around so I could reach into the back seat. That meant my butt ended up sticking straight up in the air, which Dan politely refrained from mentioning. I popped open the briefcase, grabbed the folder, and righted myself in the seat.

"Those acrobatics were pretty slick," Dan said. "When you lived in Paris, did you join the circus?"

I narrowed my eyes at him. "Yeah, I was the knife thrower." He laughed, and I opened up the folder. "You said there was something off about the center she's going to?"

"You'll see."

I flipped through the papers, the first of which was a printout of the halfway house's web page. It was called The Open Arms Center for Women and Youth, and based on the one sentence description, it was a place for homeless teen mothers.

"Is this place really appropriate for Jada?" I asked. "I don't want to come off as judgy, but this is a place for homeless kids and recovering addicts."

"I hear you, but there's a method to the madness," Dan replied. "This place is women-only, and since Jada's mentally a middle school girl, this is a better option than a coed place."

"Good point." I rifled through the papers and froze when I came on a picture of the center's front door. Above it was a stone slab with a buckle carved into it.

"There's a buckle above the doorway?" I said. "It looks exactly like the one Tessa and I found at Dim Sum Delight."

"Turns out the center's in an old historical building. Guess who owns it." Dan's gaze slid toward me. "And still makes rather large donations several times a year."

"Please don't say Nathaniel Beauclaire."

"Nope. Jacob Allwood's family has been funding it for years." Dan turned off the street, and I realized we were at the Allwood Compound's front gate. "I figured you'd want to come here next."

"You figured right."

Chapter 13

Intent And Emotion

Because Dan was with me, I couldn't sneak through the Allwood mansion like I normally did. Well, I could have, but since Dan was on the police force if anyone didn't recognize us and called the cops about a couple of intruders, that would have been awkward. Therefore, we stood in the foyer, waiting impatiently, while a servant rushed off to collect Jacob from whatever he was doing.

After a few minutes, I realized that I was the impatient one, while Dan was stiff as a board and sweating buckets in the nicely air-conditioned home. I followed his gaze; he was staring at the door to the basement he'd been held captive in a few months ago.

"Hey." I touched the back of his hand. "You okay?"

"I'm fine," he ground out.

I hooked my pinky finger around his. "Is it too weird, being here?"

"I can handle it." He laced his fingers with mine. "Let's not go into the basement, though. Deal?"

"Deal."

We were still smiling at each other when Jacob arrived, his servant hot on his heels.

"Eli, Dan, lovely to see you two together again," Jacob said. "To what do I owe the pleasure?"

"We wanted to ask you about a property your family owns," I replied.

Jacob nodded. "Intriguing, but I wouldn't expect anything less from you. Follow me."

Dan, myself, and the servant followed Jacob into his office. Jacob took his place behind his desk. Dan and I sat in the chairs across from him, while the servant stood sentry at the door.

"You can go, LeClerc," Jacob said, and the servant left the room. "I apologize for the inconvenience," Jacob said, jerking his chin toward the spot where his servant had recently been, "but a threat was recently made against my life. If only they realized what an empty threat that was," he added.

"Is everything all right? Do you need help?" I asked.

"It's nothing out of the ordinary, and nothing I can't handle," he replied. "Now, you wanted to ask me about one of my properties?"

"It's called The Open Arms Center for Women and Youth," Dan said as he placed the folder on Jacob's desk. "Tax records show your family owns the land, and has paid in excess of eighty percent of the center's expenses over the last few decades."

"Yes, I imagine they would." Jacob glanced at the folder, but didn't open it. "The short answer is that the center is one of Cecily's pet projects. Making sure young mothers and their children were cared for was a cause near to Cecily's heart. I have no intention of halting the payments, if that's what you're wondering."

"Not quite." I glanced at Dan, and continued, "The girl Sarah possessed, Jada Morales, is due to be released from the hospital on Monday. This is the center she's being transferred to."

Jacob frowned. "Yes, that is... That is quite interesting." He got up, and stood in front of the windows. "When last we spoke, you told me Jada has some memories from when she was possessed. Have any more memories returned to her?"

"I don't know. I haven't seen her since then, because I was dealing with two other possessions."

"Two?" Jacob turned around and planted his hands on his desk. "Who was behind them? Was it Sarah?"

"We don't know," I began, "but these were demonic possessions. We think it was the same entity behind both incidents. First, they took over a cook at a local restaurant, and the second possession—"

"Was me," Dan finished. "I was possessed by that dirt bag."

Jacob grunted. "Dan, would you mind if I spoke to Eliza alone for a moment?"

Dan glanced at me. After I nodded, he said, "Not at all. I'll wait in the hallway."

Once the door clicked shut behind Dan, Jacob came around his desk and sat next to me. "Are you all right?"

"I'm fine. I wasn't one of the people that got possessed."

"No, but you care a great deal for Dan, and he was."

I looked away from the insightful dead man. "What makes you think I care for him?"

"Remember, I saw the both of you in the basement, when you all but begged his spirit not to leave his body."

I remembered that day all too well; Dan had been beaten unconscious, and no matter what I said or did, he wouldn't wake up. "I had to help him."

"And you did." Jacob placed his hand on mine, and for the hundredth time, I marveled at how he felt like a flesh and blood man, instead of like a spirit. "Emotional pain is still pain. If you need to discuss what happened with someone who understands, I'm here."

"Thanks, Jacob. That means a lot." I looked toward the closed door. "Why did you ask Dan to leave?"

"Sometimes, it's easier to be honest without an audience."

"If anything, I was Dan's audience. I was there throughout the whole ordeal until I cast out the demon out of him." I looked at Jacob and sighed. "It was pretty intense."

He patted my hand. "Possessions always are." He rose and went to the door. It opened of its own accord. "You may return, Dan."

"Thanks." Dan entered the room, and the door shut behind him. "Neat trick."

"Isn't it? Have a seat."

Dan reclaimed his seat and gave me a questioning look. I shrugged, and watched as Jacob rummaged through a cabinet. He made a few trips to his desk, dropping off bottles, crystals, and a large silver tray.

"Eli, you know the basics of casting a spell, correct?"

"I do."

"You do?" Dan asked.

"Of course. What do you think Tessa and I were doing in Paris?" I approached the supplies Jacob had assembled. "What would you like me to start with?"

"Just light the incense, for now."

I poured some sand into a small stone bowl, then I set a white candle in the holder. I snapped my fingers to ignite the candle, then I held a charcoal disc over the flame and dropped it into the bowl. I waited for a tendril of smoke to curl upward, then I set an incense cone on top of the charcoal.

"That smells nice," I said. "Did you blend this yourself?"

"It's nag champa," Jacob replied. "LeClerc gets it for me at the local head shop."

I turned to Dan, and caught him trying not to laugh. He settled down when Jacob approached him with a vial of oil.

"Just going to anoint you," Jacob murmured as he used his thumb to mark Dan's forehead. "Tell me your full name."

"Daniel Edward Lyons."

"How long have you had this name?"

"Since before I was born, although my mother was originally going to call me Richard."

"What other names do you use?"

"None."

Jacob nodded. "He's not possessed."

"I told you I wasn't," Dan said.

"You can check for that?" I asked, more relieved than I'd expected to be.

"Oh, yes. It's quite simple." Jacob approached the supplies on his desk, mixed a few herbs into a mortar and pestle, and began grinding them. "Eliza, if you would, please hand me the grapeseed oil."

I passed the bottle to him and watched him add some oil to the herbs. "I thought we were casting a spell?"

Jacob glanced up and smiled. "We are. Here, hold this." He handed me a tiny glass bottle. Jacob then fitted the bottle with a funnel and poured in his herb and oil mixture. "Do you want Daniel to ever be possessed again?"

"No," I replied. "Never."

"What will you do to keep that from happening?"

"Anything in my power, and if I can't prevent it or fix it I'll find someone who can."

"Good." Having finished adding the mixture to the bottle, Jacob removed the funnel and handed me a cork. "Seal that good and tight. You'll want to anoint Dan periodically, at least every few days, to keep the anti-possession intent strong."

"Wait." I looked at the bottle in my hand. "This was the spell?"

"Of course. Witchcraft is based on intent and emotion. No one has stronger emotions about Dan than you do, therefore you only needed to state your intent." He leaned closer, and asked, "What has Tessa been teaching you about witchcraft?"

"I don't really ask her anything," I mumbled, then I thrust the bottle into my bag. I glanced at Dan, who remained silent but had heard every word. "Thank you."

"You're very welcome." Jacob moved around his supplies. "Now, onto Jada."

"Are we gonna anti-possess her, too?" Dan asked.

"We should probably craft something for the girl," Jacob replied. "In the meantime, I agree that Jada being sent to the same home Cecily once championed is suspect. I will have one of our doctors speak to those treating Jada. Hopefully, we can discover who made this arrangement, and why."

"How are you going to get her doctors to divulge that?" I asked.

"My dear, with money and magic, one can accomplish almost anything."

Dan stood and shook Jacob's hand. "Thank you, for everything."

"Again, you're quite welcome. I will send Eli a message once I have some information. We can review it together, if you'd like."

We said our goodbyes, and saw ourselves out. As we drove out of the Allwood Compound's gate, I saw a riot of bright pink blooms. There was a group of bleeding heart growing right next to Jacob's fence.

CHAPTER 14

EVERYONE HAS A LEARNING CURVE

WHILE DAN DROVE AWAY from the Allwood Compound, I typed furiously on my phone. "What are you doing?" he asked.

"I saw more bleeding hearts, and I'm checking the internet for any information I can find about them," I replied.

"Does the internet have a lot to say about bleeding hearts?"

"No," I wailed. I hadn't meant to wail. "This must mean something. These plants are popping up all over town, and it's weird."

"We'll figure it out. We're good with weird."

Dan was right. We were a good team, and we would figure this out, but mysterious these plants would have to wait for a while. The plants weren't hurting anyone—at least, not as far as I knew—and we had more pressing concerns. I dropped my phone into my bag and asked, "Where are we going?"

"I figured we'd drive by the halfway house," Dan replied. "Jada's not due to be transferred for three days. We can use this time to figure out what's happening there."

"It's Friday," I mumbled; since Dan's possession, I'd completely lost track of time. "Wait, how did you swing a three-day weekend?" I asked, since Dan usually picked up a few shifts over the weekend.

Dan smiled. "Luck of the draw. That, and I had a ton of time off that was sitting there unused." He cleared his throat and said, "So, Jacob said you have some strong emotions about me."

"Jacob's dead. What does he know?"

Dan laughed softly. "Good point."

The Open Arms Center for Women and Youth was located on the opposite side of town from the Allwood Compound, which was typical. When the witch clans had settled the area, they were the ones that had money and resources, and as such they claimed all the prime real estate. The poor mortals had to make do with whatever was leftover. For the most part, things had worked out fine, but places like transitional homes ended up in the narrow, congested streets near the canals. Even now, hundreds of years later, mortals were confined to certain areas. I wondered how many of them realized why they ended up living where they did.

Dan parked across the street from the center. "Here we are," he said. "You know, I've been by this place a hundred times, but I never noticed that giant buckle over the door."

"Has it always been there?" I wondered. The buckle was carved out of a slab of pink granite, and it had to be four feet across.

"Probably. Nowadays, a detail like that is too expensive to put on a place like this."

"I wonder how old the building is." I grabbed my phone, pulled up the town library's website, and accessed the property records division. I'd stolen login credentials a while ago, and the municipal IT department hadn't had them changed yet. "This place has been here for at least two hundred years." I pulled up another screen. "Make that three hundred, and counting. The older records haven't been scanned, not yet," I explained.

"Who was the original property owner?"

"You'll never guess." I enlarged the signature. "Jemima Allwood Beauclaire."

"Nathaniel's wife. Interesting."

"The property stayed in her name well into the eighteen hundreds, which was long after she died."

"Was it always a home?"

"Not sure." Scanned property records only revealed so much. "I wonder why Cecily was so interested in a home for unwed mothers."

"Maybe Cecily was an unwed mother, once upon a time."

"Even if she was, it would have hardly mattered. Witches are big into lineage, and the family wouldn't have disowned her over a pregnancy, planned or otherwise. They would have welcomed a new member."

"Are seers into lineage, too?"

"Yeah. It's maddening." I set down my phone, staring straight ahead at nothing. "I mean, the seer community wants me to lead them, but I'm not sure I can do that. They see me as Helena Moore's legacy, but I'm just me. I can't do half of what Gran did. No one can." I glanced at Dan, saw him watching at me. "Dad is way more qualified than I am."

"He's already got a job. You said it yourself. And while I never met your grandmother, I bet she wasn't born knowing everything." He moved so he was sideways in his seat, facing me. "Everyone has a learning curve. I bet she had one, too."

I mirrored his position. "I like this straight talk. You say the best things."

"Only you think that. Most complain I'm too blunt."

"Everyone has a learning curve. You'll get better at communicating," I said, then I saw movement out of the corner of my eye, and realized it was a spirit. No, make that spirits.

"There are a lot of ghosts attached to this place." I sat up, and watched the line of spirits file into the front entrance. "Were the children born here, too?"

Dan shrugged. "Not as far as I know, but hospital births are a relatively new phenomenon. For the first few hundred years of this building's life, if a woman went into labor here, she most likely would have given birth here."

"You know a lot about birth locations."

"Like I said, I wasn't always a cop. I wanted to be a history teacher."

I tore my gaze from the spirits back to Dan. "Really?"

"It's a fact. But I needed a job with better pay and health insurance, so I went into the academy."

He needed those things to take care of Charlotte. I leaned across the center console and kissed his stubbly cheek.

"What was that for?"

"For you being you." I settled back in my seat. "Want to talk to some ghosts with me?"

The first rule of attracting spirit attention is to do it where mortals won't notice what you're doing. Granted, most mortals would assume I was on a call, or talking to myself, but there was always one nosy person in the bunch who just had to figure out what was going on. I had better things to do than explain to a stranger why I was standing around talking to thin air.

The second rule was to remain calm, and act like the spirit couldn't cause you any harm. A spirit can absolutely harm a living being in a myriad of different ways, but most spirits were ordinary dead people who had no idea what they were capable of. Based on the old-fashioned style of clothing the spirits milling around the center were wearing, they'd been around long enough to learn a thing or two.

Dan and I exited the car, and I stood on the sidewalk waiting for them to notice me. My seer abilities acted like a beacon to spirits; Gran had always likened us to a candle blazing in the dark. Once a few saw me, and realized that I could see them, I jerked my head toward an alley and walked about halfway down. When I stopped and turned around, I learned that my plan had worked. Two spirits were following me.

"We've got company," I said, then I pushed up my sleeve and bared my seer's mark. Dan placed his palm on my mark, the contact necessary to let him see and interact with the spirits as well. We'd done it before, but this time was different.

"Whoa," Dan said as the connection flared to life between us, and the air crackled with static electricity. "Did you do that?"

"I have no idea what that was," I replied, then I turned to the spirits. "Hi. My name is Eliza. This is Dan. Is it okay if we ask you some questions about the center?"

"Wasn't no center when I was in it," the younger-appearing spirit said. "It was where embarrassments like me was sent, is all."

The older spirit shook her head. "Never you mind Alice. I'm Marion, and I was a midwife here. It was as good a place to work for a woman as you could get back then." She paused, and added, "Well, it was after Mama Cecily took over."

"By Mama Cecily, do you mean Cecily Allwood?" Dan asked.

"Yes, that's her," Marion replied. "She made sure we had plenty to eat, and clean water and sheets, and blankets for the babies. She was right good to us. We had us good lives, and it was all because of her."

"If you don't mind my asking, why are you still here? In my experience, spirits only remain earthbound when they're disgruntled, or have unfinished business, but you seem to have had a good life."

"I sure did have a good life, and you're right, our business isn't yet done. Mama Cecily made us swear to watch over this place for as long as young girls were sent to it." Marion looked toward the center, and smiled. "As you can see, we've still got work to do."

"I guess you do." I looked at Dan. He squeezed my wrist, sending another crackle of energy up my arm.

"Do you know why Miss Allwood took an interest in the center?" Dan asked. "Did she have a baby here?"

"She didn't, but," Marion leaned closer, "many years ago, she brought a girl here who had a baby soon after, a healthy girl just like her momma. We thought it might be Mama Cecily's granddaughter, but we never did find out one way or the other."

"What happened to the baby?" I asked.

"She grew up in town, and lived here, and then a town over, until around twenty years ago," Marion replied. "Her name was... was..."

"Christina," Alice said, and my blood went cold. "Her name was Christina Louise."

"Was this Christina a witch, like Cecily?" Dan asked. "She must have been if she lived that long, right?"

"Well now, I am not one to out someone," Marion said, "but I can tell you that the last time I saw Miss Christina she looked no older than Alice here. She even had a little girl of her own, and what an angelic child she was. That girl had the sweetest curls and big, beautiful eyes, and she was as pretty as a picture."

"Was she," I said, my stomach full of butterflies. I didn't know if Dan could pick up on what I was feeling through our connection, so I tugged my hand away. "Thank you for your help, ladies. I really appreciate it."

"You're most welcome, Miss Eliza."

Marion and Alice returned to the center. I watched them walk away, then I turned to Dan. "I'm freaking out a bit here."

"Let's get back to the car."

Dan took my hand, careful to avoid my mark, and we walked back to the car. He even opened the door for me. After he'd driven a few blocks away from the center, he said, "Talk to me, babe."

"Why do you keep calling me babe?"

"Eliza. What happened?"

I took a deep breath. "My mother's name is Christina Louise, and she lived a town over until about twenty years ago."

SECRET HANDSHAKE

"That is one hell of a coincidence," Dan said. "Do you think this baby Marion mentioned could also be your mother?"

"I have no idea. I mean, I literally have no idea." I slid down in the seat and covered my face with my hands. "All I know about my mother is her name, and that she wasn't really interested in being a parent, and that she moved away when I was eight. That's about it."

"You never tried to find her?"

"What's the point? If she didn't want to be around me when I was a kid, she won't want to be around me now." I laughed through my nose. "I guess Jada and me have more in common than I realized."

"Was your mother a witch?"

"I..." I took a breath, started again. "I was about to say, of course not, but I don't really know the answer to that, either."

"Would Tessa know?"

"I don't remember Tessa and my mother spending a lot of time together. In fact, Mom stayed as far away from Gran and Dad as she could. It's why we didn't live in town. She worried Gran would influence me."

"But if she was a witch, Tessa would know, right?"

I faced Dan. "Exactly how would Tessa know? Secret handshake?"

He shrugged. "Magic?"

"There's no way to sense if another human is witchborn or not. You either have to have a charm, like my witchfinder, or wait until you catch them using magic."

"I wonder why she kept her distance." Dan glanced at me. "Her last name wasn't Allwood, was it?"

"No. Lind."

"You were never Eliza Lind?"

"No. Even in kindergarten I was Eli Moore."

"I bet you were a cute kid."

"You know it." Dan made a right turn and headed into the downtown area. Standing at the main intersection were the Ghost Guys.

"Them again," I muttered. "They are the three most incompetent humans I've ever encountered."

"Or they just want to seem that way. Got your witchfinder on you?"

"You don't think they're—well, I guess anything's possible." I fished my witchfinder out of my bag while Dan drove around the block. By the time he came around to the intersection again, I had the amulet clutched in my fist. The Ghost Guys were still at the corner, waving their useless equipment around and irritating pedestrians.

I rolled down the window and said, "Hey, guys. Still looking for the undead?"

"It's you," Mike said, once again inordinately happy to see me. "And your detective friend! Are you two on a mission?"

"Always," I said. The light turned green, and Dan drove off, leaving the Ghost Guys to wonder what we were up to.

"Get anything off them?" Dan asked.

I opened my hand. The witchfinder hadn't heated up, but there was a pale blue glow around it. "They're not witches, but they're using some kind of magic." I turned and watched them through the rear window. "Do you think their hokey equipment might be on to something?"

"Next time we see them—and I'm sure they'll turn up again—we'll ask them when and why they came here. Gotta be a trail. We just need to follow it."

"Yeah." I faced forward, still clutching the witchfinder. "Just have to follow it."

CHAPTER 16

TIME FOR A BREAK

MY THOUGHTS RACED, JUMPING from my mother, to the Ghost Guys, to wondering how everything tied all together. When I looked up, I realized Dan had driven us to the center of town. "Where are we going?"

"We are taking a break," Dan replied. "This has been a hell of a day, what with going to your grandmother's house, then Jacob's haunted mansion, the women's home, and those ghost clowns are the icing on the cake. We need to decompress."

"No argument here."

"I mean, I saw ghost cats. I *pet* a ghost cat!"

"They're good kitties, and they're great judges of character. Consider it an honor that Pumpkin let you pet her."

"Oh, believe me, I do." Dan parked in one of the marked spaces on Main Street, then he got out paid the automatic parking meter. He came back and set the ticket on the dashboard, and said, "Let's go."

"Okay." I got out and looked up and down the street. "Where to?"

"A walk, for starters," he replied. "When I first transferred to this department, and things got heavy fast, I used to come down here and wander the streets."

"Isn't that called loitering?"

"Nah. Loitering is when you stay in one place. I was in motion. Anyway, I would come here, walk around for a while, and think about everything. Sometimes, I thought about nothing. Usually, it helped."

"And when it didn't?"

"That's when I busted out my secret weapon." Dan pushed the walk button. We waited for the light to change, then we hurried across the street.

"What is this weapon?"

"Not a what. A place." We walked under a wrought iron arch into the court-yard alongside city hall. I don't know if I'd call the spot a park, but the tall hedges meant the traffic noises were muffled, and the well-kept walkways and benches were a good place to hide out from the world, if only for a little while.

"Is this your secret hideout? I asked.

He smiled. "I guess it is." We sat on one of the benches. I could see city hall's roofline looming over the hedge. From this angle, it resembled a castle. "When things were tough I would sit here, and think—or not think, if that's what I needed. Sitting here never fixed anything, but it's nice to escape from your problems every now and then."

"It is," I said, then I leaned back and turned my face toward the sun. I still had the witchfinder clutched in my hand, and I could feel the residue of whatever magic it had picked up. The longer I held it, the more I was convinced that the residue was familiar. I had either encountered this specific magic before, or I was familiar with the person who wielded it.

We heard a creaky old carnival tune in the distance. An ice cream truck was approaching. "Be right back," Dan said, then he went in search of the music's source. I watched him disappear beyond the hedge, then I opened my hand and looked at the witchfinder. The magic had congealed around the amulet into a gritty blue slime. I worried at it with my thumb, and it balled up like dried rubber cement. I held the blue ball of goo between my thumb and forefinger and squinted at it.

"Who made you?" I asked the magic goo. Unsurprisingly, it remained silent.

I dropped the blue ball onto the cement sidewalk and watched it roll to the opposite side of the pavement and come to rest against a decorative column. The carvings on the column featured two torches with an ornamental swag between them, which reminded me of the gate to the Père Lachaise cemetery in Paris. I tilted my head back and closed my eyes, remembering all the times I'd visited the cemetery with Dad. When I returned to Paris years later with Tessa, she hadn't been as interested in visiting the dead, which was understandable. As seers, Dad and I felt obligated to make sure the cemetery's occupants were at rest, but witches didn't have that sort of call, except for their ancestors.

Then Amir came to visit me for my birthday, and he was willing to go anywhere I wanted in the city, legalities and treaties be damned. I remember one time, when we crept past the *Aux Morts* memorial after midnight...

I heard a ping, and felt a jolt against my palm. I looked down and saw the witchfinder had cracked in two. That break didn't have a natural explanation, since the amulet was a solid silver ornament without any seams to loosen or pry apart... Which meant there was a magical explanation.

The blue slime was stretched across the broken planes of the amulet, confirming my theory that magic had done this. Jacob had reminded me that magic was based on intent and emotion, which meant the slime had picked up on what I was feeling. I'd been thinking about the time Amir and I broke into an ossuary—

Shit.

I'd been thinking about Amir, and the blue slime cracked my witchfinder in half.

"Babe."

Dan was walking toward me, an ice cream cone in each hand. "Chocolate or strawberry?"

"Strawberry," I said, and I dropped my witchfinder into my bag. Dan's eyes tracked the movement.

"What happened?" he asked.

"Remember how I mentioned my ex?" I licked the ice cream. It was more vanilla than strawberry, but it was cold and delicious.

"That Amir guy? Yeah."

"I think he's behind the Ghost Guys."

CHAPTER 17

STAY

Tessa shook her head. "I don't like it."

"Neither do I, but what other explanation is there?" I demanded. Dan and I had gone back to my apartment, where Tessa had been whiling away the time eating cookies and scheduling clients. Her day definitely took a turn for the worse after we told her what we'd been up to, and I showed her my broken witchfinder. "The Ghost Guys show up out of nowhere and find me in a random alley, then their leader shows up here on a lame spirit quest. Then I have the witchfinder out near them, and this blue gunk appears. These clues are starting to point toward Amir."

Tessa picked at the blue residue on the amulet, just like I had. "I don't remember Amir's magic feeling blue."

"Magic has a color?" Dan asked, from where he leaned against the kitchen counter.

"More of a feel, but yes," Tessa replied. "Have you ever seen one of those acts where a psychic will show the audience an individual's aura? Magic is similar to an aura. Its color and brightness vary from person to person."

Dan grunted. "And Amir's is not blue?"

"He's more of an orange," Tessa replied. "He has a lot of anger, with undertones of inadequacy."

"Maybe the blue is from one of the Ghost Guys," I offered. "But I was thinking about Amir when the witchfinder cracked. And before that, I scraped off some of the residue and dropped it on the ground. The residue rolled toward a column that looks just like the ones at the entrance to Père Lachaise."

Tessa's brow pinched. "When you say you were thinking about Amir, exactly what were you remembering?"

"Um." I glanced at Dan, and almost asked him to leave the room. "The time we broke into the ossuary."

"You what?" Dan demanded. "You broke into a house of bones?"

"Yes, we did," I said, then I turned to Tess. "I was thinking about how we beat the enchantment on the door."

"I rescind my argument," Tessa said. "This has Amir written all over it."

"Because it's blue?" Dan asked.

"Because the magic they used to break the ossuary's enchantment was blue, and when they did break it, the metal door cracked like an egg." Tessa set the amulet on the table. "Why would he send his cronies here now?"

"I don't know." I held my head in my hands. "It's been three years since we broke up, and I haven't heard from him at all. Now, this." I straightened. "This isn't about me. Amir has some other game in town, and tormenting me is just his fun side gig. We need to figure out why he's really here."

"Maybe Alex knows," Dan said. "Think he's awake yet?"

Tessa blinked. "Alex is here?"

"He got in this morning, and Dad sleeps for days when he gets home," I replied. "If we're lucky, he'll be coherent by Monday."

"Dan may be on to something," Tessa said. "Alex follows the magical tides around the world. What if whatever drew him here was Amir's doing?"

"Dad didn't mention anything like that," I said. "He said he came home because he missed me."

"Both of those things can be true at the same time," Tessa said.

Dan pushed off the counter, turned one of the kitchen chairs around backward, and straddled it. "Table Alex's motivations for now. This Amir sounds like bad news."

"Yes," I said, while Tessa said, "Oh, most definitely." I gave Tess some side eye, but she was right. If there was trouble happening, Amir was invariably at its nexus.

"What if Amir is behind all of the random bleeding hearts popping up all over town?" I asked.

"Gods below, I hope not," Tessa muttered. "Besides, flowers aren't Amir's style. He fancies himself a crime boss, or a ruthless emperor. Even though he's powerful, he sends others to do his work for him. Doesn't want to dirty his hands," she added.

"They must have gotten plenty dirty in an ossuary," Dan said.

"That was different. He only wanted to break into the ossuary because he wanted to see if I could do it." I leaned back and stared at the ceiling. "You could say he was grooming me. He wanted to understand the full extent of my abilities, in order to assess if I was worth bringing into the fold."

"Grooming," Dan repeated, then he said to Tessa, "I thought you were with her in Paris. How could you let that happen?"

"When we went to Paris, Eli was twenty-four and an adult," Tessa replied. "Therefore, while we were there, Eli did not need or require my permission to do anything or see anyone."

"Eli concurs," I said.

"Still, you were awful young," Dan said, but Tessa shook her head.

"When I was twenty-four, I was already on my second marriage, was the de facto head of my clan, and I ruled a large swath of Italy in the process," she added.

"You... ruled?"

She smiled sweetly. "Tessa is short for Contessa Isabella della Scala. You will note that nowhere in my name or title is the word babysitter."

"Point taken," Dan said, then he slid his hand across the table and touched my forearm. "What else did this Amir have you do?"

I shrugged. "Nothing I didn't want to do."

"You say that a lot."

"What does that mean?"

"It means you get pushed around a lot by these magical jerks."

"They're not all jerks!"

"Have your lovers' spat later," Tessa said, then she stood. "Actually, have it now. I'm going to talk to Alex."

With that, Tessa walked out the door. I stared at it for a moment, then I said, "I didn't feel like we were having a spat."

"Maybe not, but I upset you." Dan took both of my hands in his. "What I meant was, things get done to you. You said Amir didn't have you do anything you didn't want to do, and when I was possessed, and we…" He cleared his throat. "You said the same thing. Are you sure you wanted to do any of that?"

"Yes. I-I think so." I unwound myself from him and covered my face with my hands. "It's just that everything I like always crashes down around me, and I have to hold on to the good, you know? When we were together, it was good. I felt good. And then it wasn't even you."

"Hey. Hey." Dan came around the table and crouched in front of me. "I'm so sorry, Eli. I've been coming on strong, and I should have eased off. I don't want to make this hard for you."

"It's not hard. It's awful." I wiped my face with the shoulder of my shirt. "And you didn't even do anything wrong. You're the victim here."

"We're both victims, but if me being near you hurts you, say the words and I'll go."

I peeked up at him. "You would? But I thought you wanted to be with me."

"I do, but not if it hurts you." He caressed the side of my face, his palm coming to rest on my cheek. "God, Eli, I could never hurt you."

"I could never hurt you, either." I put my hand on top of his. "Stay?"

He nodded. "I'll stay, as long as you want me to."

CHAPTER 18

THE LYONS FAMILY ESTATE

DAN AND I SPENT Friday night on my couch, eating takeout and watching movies on my laptop. I'd never really gotten into pop culture, but he had an encyclopedic knowledge of every science fiction movie, television show, and animated series that had been released in the last thirty years. Not so long ago, I'd thought being a police officer was his life, but he kept surprising me. I liked surprises.

I must have fallen asleep before Dan, because I woke up in bed, alone. I grabbed my phone to call him and heard his ringing from out in the office. A moment later, Dan appeared in the bedroom doorway.

"Hey," I said, tossing the phone onto the bed. "Did you watch movies all night?"

"I, ah, slept on the couch."

"That could not have been comfortable." I almost asked why he had moved me into the bedroom, or why he hadn't slept in the bed with me, but the reason was obvious. He thought I needed space, and he was giving it to me. And they said chivalry was dead.

"It was fine." He glanced at the windows. "The sun's barely up. Do you always get up this early?"

"Only in summer. I like to run before it gets too hot." I looked over his sleep-rumpled outfit; he wasn't dressed for running, and I didn't have anything that would fit him. Well, I did have his tee shirt and sweatpants from the other day, but they were still in the laundry basket. "Want to go for a walk?"

He yawned. "Sure."

"Great." I tossed the comforter aside. "I'm going to make some coffee, so it'll be ready when we get back."

I padded into the kitchen and set up the coffeemaker. When I returned to the bedroom, Dan was sprawled out on my bed, fast asleep. I moved to wake him, then I remembered how much I'd enjoyed snuggling with him on the couch, both last night and a few days ago at his place. He'd fallen asleep that time at his place, too, and I realized how hard he'd been pushing himself. He'd been running himself ragged, all for me.

One morning's worth of sleeping in won't kill me. I crawled back into bed, pulled the comforter up to my chin, and let myself drift off.

When I opened my eyes again, sunlight was streaming into the room, the scent of coffee was wafting in from the kitchen, and Dan was spooning me. I took a moment to bask in the luxury of being warm and safe and held, wondering if I could bottle these feelings so I could whip them out as needed. I wasn't kidding when I told Dan that good things never last for me, and I needed to hold on to whatever I could.

I rolled over so I was facing him. I tried not to jostle him awake, but let's face it, this was no princess and the pea situation. Dan blinked his eyes open and smiled at me.

"Hey."

"Hey."

"Still want to go for a walk?"

"We can walk later."

The corner of his mouth curled up, then he pushed my hair back from my cheek. "Your eyes are so dark," he murmured. "Even in the sunlight."

"My grandfather, he was Indian," I said. "Gran used to say I had his eyes."

"I guess she would know." Dan kept stroking my hair. "What are you thinking?"

"About how different this is compared to the last time we woke up in bed together," I replied. "I like the real you."

"I like remembering what my body does, and where it's been," he said, and I laughed.

"Me, too." I moved closer to him, and laid my head on his chest. "It was fun being naked, though."

Dan threaded his fingers through my hair. "I can make that happen."

I propped myself up on my elbow and glowered at him. "I'm sure you can." Dan's eyes widened, and I worried I'd taken our teasing too far. Then his hand slid down my back and lifted up the bottom of my shirt, and I froze. All I could think about was waking up in Dan's bed, and the smug stare of the demon inside his body.

What if he's possessed again?

"Hey. Hey." Dan sat up, taking me with him. "We're just teasing each other, right?"

"R-Right. Let's eat breakfast."

I got out of bed and went into the kitchen without a backward glance. When I was reaching for the cereal bowls, Dan leaned against the counter next to me.

"Are we okay?" he asked.

"Yes." I put down the bowls and faced him. "That was my fault. I'm sorry."

"Don't be. We were just talking."

"For a second, I remembered how the demon had looked at me, and…" I crossed my arms over my stomach. "I was scared you were possessed again."

Dan wrapped his arms around me. "It's me. Promise."

"That's exactly what a possessed guy would say."

He chuckled. "I guess you're right. Does that mean I get the salt treatment again?"

I smiled against his chest, since the fact that he remembered me using the salt to drive out the demon meant he was, in fact, my Dan. "I believe you, for now, but I've got my eye on you, Lyons."

"Yes, ma'am."

He helped me set the table, and we enjoyed a hearty breakfast of hot coffee and cold cereal.

"You're off today, too, right?" I asked.

"That I am," he replied. "What do you want to do today? Lay low?"

"That sounds fantastic. Although I don't really want to be here."

"I thought you liked it here." He looked around the kitchen. "It's a nice apartment."

"It is, but not if you want to be left alone. Everyone who's looking for me will come here first. Nathaniel has been known to drop by, and now we have the stupid Ghost Guys to worry about. Even Bennet comes by on a whim. I need to be away from all of that, at least for now."

"Okay," Dan said. "Where to? Your grandmother's?"

"Not if Tessa's there with a bone to pick with Dad."

"I take it they have a history?"

"Do they ever." I shoved a few things into my bag, including the broken witchfinder. Even though it was in pieces, it probably still worked. "You'd think they'd be over it by now, but they love dragging up the past."

"Over what? Were they a couple?" Dan asked, and I nodded. "What happened?"

"My mother happened." I put my empty mug and bowl in the sink. "Ready?" Dan opened the door. "Where to?"

"Your place." I hadn't known I was going to say that until the words fell out of my mouth, but it was done. "You promised me a tour."

And that was how I ended up at Dan's house for the third time in a week. Was it stressful or awkward to be in the same house where Dan had been possessed, pleasured me, and then showed me his dead wife's photo albums? No, not at all. I always clench my jaw this tightly.

But, I would rather be here with Dan than dealing with Nathaniel Beauclaire's latest mischief, and whatever the Ghost Guys and Amir were up to. I also preferred this to being at Gran's while Tess and Dad did their eternal exes-who-are-still-in-love dance. If the universe was of a mind to be kind to me, I could hide out here just long enough to organize my thoughts and get a game plan together for at least one of my ever-growing list of problems. But, the universe does not have a mind, isn't kind, and could care less about my happiness.

Maybe I could just build a blanket fort and stay there. Permanently.

"Here we are," Dan said as he opened the front door. "Since you want the grand tour, we'll start here in the front hall. The realtor that sold this place to us called it a foyer, but I don't like that word."

"Why? Not manly enough?"

Dan's gaze slid toward me. "Smartass. As you can see, the front hall opens into the living room. Through that doorway," Dan pointed toward the far side of the room, "is the kitchen, dining room, and the guest bathroom. To the left is the downstairs bedroom and full bath, but you already knew that part."

I narrowed my gaze. "Funny, Dan. Real funny."

"I'm considering a second career in stand up. Hang on a sec."

Dan disappeared down the hall. A bare two minutes later he was back, pulling a fresh shirt over his head.

"A comedian and a quick-change artist. Impressive." I walked to the base of the stairs. "What's up there?"

"The master suite, spare bedrooms that I use for storage, all that jazz," Dan replied. "Like you said, this place is way too big for me."

"If the master suite's up there, why do you—"

And I shut my mouth, since he probably hadn't slept up there since Charlotte died. "I mean, it's your house. You can sleep wherever you want."

"I know what you're thinking, and you're partially correct. I moved into the downstairs bedroom while Charlotte was still alive, to give her space. She had a lot of assistive devices," he added. "After she was gone, I stayed down here." He put his foot on the bottom step and extended his hand to me. "Come on. I know you want to check out every nook and cranny."

"You're okay with this?"

"I am okay with this."

I took his hand, and we ascended to the second floor of Dan's picture perfect family friendly house. The butterflies in my stomach had moved past fluttering and were organizing a full on stampede.

Halfway up the staircase was a landing. "Oh, this is much manlier than the entryway," I said.

"You know it."

We arrived at the second floor, and the first two stops off the hall were the spare bedrooms. I stuck my head into each, and discovered that one of the rooms was mostly empty, while the other was Dan's home gym, complete with a weight set and stationary bike. The third stop was another bathroom, then Dan led me to the end of the hall, and the master suite.

Holy cow, it was gorgeous.

The room was huge, easily twice as big as the downstairs bedroom Dan currently slept in. The king sized bed was situated against the far wall, and two of the walls were taken up by windows. On one side of the bed was a walk-in closet. Through the other open door I saw white and blue tile, and went to investigate the bathroom. In it was a bathtub the size of a kiddie pool.

"This tub is amazing," I said, as I perched on the side. "It has massaging jets?"

"It does, but who knows if it still works. I haven't used this thing in years."

"Well, we are going to change that." I had visions of spending the afternoon in this gorgeous tub with bubbles up to the ceiling. "It's going to be bath bombs for days around here."

"Whatever you say."

I opened my mouth to make a crack about how we might as well take baths together since we'd already been in the shower, and shut it. Not only were my wisecracks not funny, they weren't helping me or Dan sort through everything that had happened.

"I have to say, this has been a great tour." I exited the bathroom, gave the bed a wide berth, then I pivoted and entered the walk-in closet. It was completely empty.

"Not much to see in here," Dan said, as he leaned on the doorframe.

"Yeah," I said, with a sigh of relief. "I was momentarily terrified that I would walk in here and find all of Charlotte's clothes perfectly preserved."

Dan laughed softly. "That stuff has been gone for a long time. Even the furniture's new. I got rid of the old stuff, hoping it would help me move on."

"Did it help?"

"A bit." He extended his hand, and I clasped it. He pulled me toward him and out of the closet. I was still a bit on edge, so I passed him and went to check out the view.

"These windows are gorgeous." I approached the wall of windows, which overlooked the backyard. I pointed at a corner of chain link fence that wasn't attached to anything, and asked, "What's that?"

"That is the beginning of a batting cage." He stood behind me and slid his arms around my waist, resting his chin on my shoulder. "Back when I thought this would be the Lyons Family Estate, I had ideas of ball games in the back. There's enough space for an infield."

"What's back there?" The far side of Dan's yard was bordered by a stockade fence. Beyond it was a field dotted with a few scrabbly trees and shrubs.

"Last I checked, the city owned that lot."

"But you looked into buying it."

"How'd you know?"

I twisted around so I could see his face. "For the outfield, of course."

"You know me well," he said, then he kissed me. It was the first time we'd kissed all morning, and while I still wanted space to think about us, I couldn't deny how much I loved being in his arms. When we parted we went back to gazing at the yard.

"You can still make the infield," I said. "It wouldn't even be that much work. I can help, if you want."

He tightened his arms around me. "But who will play here?"

"I'm sure we can find players." Dan kissed the curve where my neck met my shoulder, so of course I started babbling. "We should start by getting those square white things that sit on the ground."

"Square white—do you mean bases?" he asked, laughing. "Wait, you do know this is for baseball, right? You have heard of baseball?"

"Yes, I've heard of baseball," I said, then I saw movement in the lot beyond Dan's property... and I recognized the people doing the moving. "Dan."

"Yeah, babe?"

"The Ghost Guys are nosing around your back fence."

Chapter 19

Ellie

"What the hell are they doing back there?" Dan demanded.

"They appear to be lost." Each one of the Ghost Guys was holding their supposed ghost hunting devices out at arm's length or up over their heads, and they consulted said devices every few moments. "Are they looking at a map?"

"Whatever their deal is, I'm getting rid of them." Dan pulled away, presumably so he could go out back and give the Ghost Guys a piece of his mind.

"Wait." I grabbed his arm. "What if they're not tracking ghosts? What if they really are tracking me?"

Dan's brows lowered, then he looked toward the Ghost Guys. "Would your ex send them after you?"

"Yes." I turned back to the window and watched the Ghost Guys bumble around the vacant lot. "Amir's style is to create chaos, then swoop in and pretend he's the savior. It took me a while to realize he was the one creating all the drama."

"If these ghost clowns are the best he has to offer, he's not all that scary," Dan said, but I shook my head.

"He is capable of amazing, terrible, and awful things," I said. "For the most part, seers don't handle magic, other than our dealings with the dead. We leave magic to the witches, but not Amir." I touched the cool windowpane. "Actually, his magic use is how we met."

"Come away from the window." Dan tossed a final glare toward the wooded lot for good measure, then he led me to the bed. I perched on the edge while Dan stood in front of me, his stance wide and his arms crossed over his chest. "How did Amir using magic make you end up meeting each other?"

"My father visits clans all over the world, renewing treaties," I began. "Witches and seers have used them for centuries. They outline what each clan can and cannot do, when to offer aid to other clans or even mortals, stuff like that. It's all pretty medieval."

"I would think someone like Bennet would handle that."

"Shepherds keep the treaties, but only a witch or a seer can renew or renegotiate one. Since Dad is Gran's only child, he's the only one qualified to act on behalf of the seers."

"He's one guy, but he deals with all of the witch clans?" Dan shook his lead. "That seems a little lopsided."

"There aren't any other options, at least not now. There aren't very many seers, and no one is as high up in the hierarchy as Dad."

"Except you."

"Yeah. Except me." I picked at the quilt. "Not all of the witch clans have treaties with us, either. Anyway, Amir decided he wanted to study magic and ended up violating the treaty. It took Dad almost six months to smooth things over."

"Amir is a seer?" Dan asked, and I nodded. "Was he punished for acting up?"

"Not really. He convinced everyone that he hadn't meant any harm and was just testing his abilities. I don't think Dad fell for it, but the witches were satisfied, so he let it drop."

"And now the creep might be here, seeing what you're up to," Dan said, in a gross oversimplification of my and Amir's relationship. "Before, you said you and Alex were in Iran because of some portals remaining open. Did Amir's studies have anything to do with these portals?"

It all came rushing back to me: the tribunals; the endless hikes over rocky, dusty terrain; the black, swirling maw of the portal. "Yeah. He had opened one of the closed ones."

"Do you know why that portal was closed?"

I shook my head. "No, but I know it had been closed over a one hundred years ago. Dad will remember why it was shut down."

"And, it's closed now?"

"Oh, yeah. Permanently closing it was one of the conditions the witches set forth. Otherwise, they wouldn't have renewed their treaty with us."

Dan grunted. "This portal must have been closed for a good reason. But that doesn't tell us why Amir is here now."

"He's smooth, and he's sneaky," I said. "Since he's not here trying to talk us into something, that mean he's sneaking around behind our backs. The Ghost Guys are probably a distraction from whatever he's really up to."

"But what would he be distracting us from," Dan said, then his eyes lit up. "Jada."

"Why Jada?"

"Amir wants power, and Jada may have an inside line on Beauclaire and his crazy mother-in-law." Dan closed the curtains, shutting out the Ghost Guys' prying eyes. "Let's pay her a visit."

We went directly from Dan's house to the hospital. Since we were both on the approved visitors list, we had no problems getting into Jada's ward. The problems began when we got to her room, and she wasn't in it.

"Where would she have gone?" I felt panic rise in my throat, terrified that Jada had been kidnapped. The edges of my vision darkened, but before I succumbed to my fears, Dan put his hand on my shoulder.

"Let's ask someone," Dan said, then he went in search of a hospital employee. I took a breath and watched him walk toward the nurses' station like the calm, un-ruffleable detective he was. I could use some of his calmness.

Actually, I suspected I was using some of his calm. I'd only had one anxiety attack since that day Dan and I rescued each other in the Allwoods' basement, and that was when Dan was possessed. Every other time I've felt myself falling into the dark hole of memory, Dan somehow pulled me back. I was grateful for the help, but I couldn't figure out how he was helping me.

A circle unbroken. Maybe we were still feeding each other energy, like Jacob had observed on that day in the basement. But how were we doing that? And why?

Dan approached the floor's reception desk. My speculations would have to wait, for now. "Excuse me, do you know where Jada Morales might be?" he asked the nurse on duty. "She's not in her room."

"Her boyfriend came by to visit, and they went for a walk," the floor nurse replied.

"Boyfriend," I repeated. "Did they leave the hospital?"

"Oh, no," she said. "Jada's not allowed to leave the hospital grounds until after she's discharged on Monday. They went out to the residents' garden."

"Thank you," I said brightly, since it wasn't the nurse's fault Jada might have been kidnapped by a power hungry seer like Amir, or possibly a lunatic ancient witch like Nathaniel.

Dan and I were quiet as we jogged back down all the flights of steps we'd just climbed up. The elevator may have been the faster option, but you don't want to find yourself in an enclosed space with someone like Amir nearby. I'd learned that lesson the hard way.

We burst into the courtyard a few minutes later, scanning the paths and benches for Jada. Since this garden was specifically made for patients and it only had one exit, Jada had to be here, unless Amir had figured out how to walk through walls, turn invisible, or magically change Jada's appearance. None of those developments would surprise me.

"There she is," Dan said, pointing toward the fountain. Jada was sitting on the edge, twirling a single red rose in her hand. Thank all the gods, she was alone.

"Hi, Jada," I called. She turned and waved, and I sat next to her. Dan kept a lookout on the other side of the fountain. "How's it going?"

"Good. You just missed Nathaniel. He brought me a flower." She held up the rose.

"Very pretty," I said. I noticed that the rose's stem had been stripped clean of thorns. "Monday's the big day, huh?"

"I can't wait," she said. "I feel like I've been cooped up in here my entire life. I'm ready to move on."

"I bet. What are your plans for after you're discharged? Do you still want me to bring you by your family's place?"

"Maybe. I don't know." Jada yanked off a few petals. "I mean, they don't seem to want to talk to me. Maybe I should respect their wishes and stay away."

"Then we won't visit." Jada peeked up at me. "You'll make a new family."

"Can I do that?"

"It's what I've been doing my whole life."

Jada glanced over her shoulder and asked, "Is that how you ended up with Detective Lyons?"

"I-I wouldn't say I'm with him," I began, and she giggled. "Not like how you're with Nathaniel, anyway."

Jada blushed. "He's been so good to me, staying close even through all of this. I'm lucky to have him."

"And he's lucky to have you." I stood, avoiding the heap of rose petals Jada had dropped onto the ground. "I won't keep you any longer, but call me on Monday, okay? After you're settled in at the new place we can go out for lunch or something."

"That would be great. Thank you, Ellie."

I froze; there was no way she could know that name. No one had called me Ellie back when we were kids, and no one had called me that for more than two years. I plastered on a smile, and said, "Welcome! Call me if you need anything."

I walked back to Dan, and together we walked in silence out of the hospital and to the parking lot. Once we were inside Dan's car, I said, "Amir was here. He's the one masquerading as her boyfriend."

"You're certain?"

"You know how everyone calls me Eli, even Bennet and my dad? Amir never did. He always called me Ellie." I faced Dan. "Jada just called me Ellie."

Dan started the car. "All right. What do we do about this?"

"Jada said her family won't talk to her. Can you see if anything happened that got the police involved?"

"I can do that today. I can run her immediate family too, look for patterns. This Amir, what's his surname?"

"Hassan."

"You met him in Iran? Is he an Iranian citizen?"

"British, actually. He was born in London."

Dan nodded. "That's enough for me to start a trace on him. I'll start a trace on the Ghost Guys, too."

"What will that do?"

"If Hassan came into this country illegally, maybe we can drown him in paperwork and buy ourselves some time."

"I don't think paperwork will slow him down," I began, then my phone pinged. I pulled it out and read a text from Tessa.

Tessa: Come to Helena's. Alex has information.
Eli: We're on our way.

CHAPTER 20

THAT CAKE WAS AWFUL

WHEN WE GOT TO Gran's house, it was already midafternoon. I went straight inside, while Dan stayed in the car and called Amir and the Ghost Guy's information into the station. I wondered if other police detectives worked constantly, or if the other officers thought Dan needed a break as much as I did. After we had this situation with Amir behind us, I might hide Dan's work phone for a few days, or weeks.

I found Tessa in the kitchen, sitting alone at the table. "Where's Dad?"

"Alex is showering." My face must have betrayed my horror, because Tessa continued, "Get those assumptions out of your head now. Alex and I haven't had that sort of relationship for decades."

"Thank the gods for that. Although you'd probably be a cool stepmother."

"I would send you to your room, lock the door and throw away the key."

"I can pick that lock in a hot second." As much fun as it was trading verbal barbs with Tessa, we had other issues. "Amir went to see Jada."

"How do you know he was there?" Tessa demanded. "Did you see him?"

"No, but Jada called me Ellie. No one has ever called me Ellie, except Amir." I sat across from Tessa and held my head in my hands. "Why is he here now?"

Tessa pursed her lips. "Alex will tell you."

I raised my head. "Dad knows?"

I heard Dan come in through the mudroom. The cats—who hadn't even lifted a paw when I arrived—stampeded down from the second floor to greet him and demand their share of attention.

"You guys ignored me and ran straight to Dan?" I called after them. "Traitors."

"Cats are the most fickle of animals," Tessa said.

"What does Dad know?" I asked. When Tessa wouldn't meet my eyes, I continued, "Is it really bad?"

She looked at me and sighed. "It's not really bad, not yet, but it's not good, either."

"Great."

Dan entered the kitchen, trailed by the Feline Federation. "Either they like me, or they're trying to kill me."

"They like you," Dad said as he entered from the opposite side of the room. His hair was still wet, and his outfit of faded jeans and an old concert tee made him look more like a college kid than someone who'd been the seers' marksman for the past fifty years. But Dad used a lot of magic, and one of the side effects of prolific spellwork was that your body and mind stayed youthful for a longer time. Gran had called it the long, golden afternoon of mystical maturity.

I glanced at Tessa. For her to look as young as she did, she must have a current of magic running through her at all times.

"If they didn't like you, you'd know," Dad continued, then he bent over and hugged me. "How are you doing, Bug?"

"Are you keeping things from me?" I countered. "Things like Amir creeping around?"

"He's not creeping, and I am not hiding anything from you." Dad went to the coffeemaker, grabbed the carafe and four mugs, and brought them to the table. "Tess, could you get the milk?"

Tessa pursed her lips at Dad, then she retrieved the milk and set it on the table. While Dad filled and handed out mugs, he said, "I honestly thought I would arrive home long before Amir got here. I'm sorry I mistimed things."

"He's been here at least a week," Dan said. "That's when the ghost clowns showed up."

"Ghost... clowns?" Dad asked, and we explained who the Ghost Guys were. When I got to the part about them scoping out the vacant lot behind Dan's house, Tessa kicked me under the table.

"Stop it," I hissed.

"Why were you there?" she hissed back.

"I ran a trace on their leader, one Michael Delacorte," Dan continued, ignoring Tessa's and my side conversation. "He first used a credit card in town nine days ago to book a couple of hotel rooms. Interesting thing is this guy's never been a high wage earner, yet his card's got a fifty thousand dollar limit, and he's staying in the most expensive place in town."

"Amir gave him the card," I said. "He must have."

Dad stared at Dan, then asked, "You can learn all of that with a single phone call?"

"Dan's a police detective," I said. "They have ways."

Dad shook his head. "That's unnerving."

"Says the guy who talks to the dead." Pumpkin hopped onto Dan's lap, purring. "These Ghost Guys have been showing up everywhere Eli goes."

"And now Amir's got Jada convinced they're in a relationship." I glanced at Dad. "How would she fit into whatever Amir's doing? Which you still haven't explained, by the way."

"Forgive me my lackadaisical attitude," Dad said. "A few months ago, Bennet began contacting seers and the allied witches across the globe, making your intent to step into Ma's position known. I support you one hundred percent." His brow pinched, and he asked, "You know that, right?"

"I do," I said in a small voice. I cleared my throat and added, "Really. I do."

Dad smiled, but it didn't reach his eyes. "I know I've failed you in many ways—"

"You haven't!"

"But I do aim to change that," he finished. "Regardless, every seer and witch I spoke with supported your claim—but those in London remained quiet. I thought that odd, since they'd always been some of Ma's most ardent supporters. I set out for London immediately, and learned was that Amir had taken over the city's witch clans, and had them and every seer in England under his control."

"Can I ask a dumb mortal question?" Dan asked.

"No question is dumb," Dad said. "Please. Ask what you'd like."

Dan glanced at Tessa, and asked, "How can a seer take over a witch?"

"Many ways," Tessa muttered. "Being that seers walk the line between life and death, and we witches try to maintain a strong bond with our ancestors, seers can use the dead against us."

"That's pretty heavy," Dan said.

"Your experience with seers is limited to Eli, and now Alex," Tessa said. "Helena had a strict code of ethics, which she taught to all of her descendants and enforced in anyone under her rule. Not everyone had the benefit of her upbringing."

"Gran was one in a million," I said. "It's why I don't want to take her place. Who could?"

"You can," Dad said. "I believe in you, and almost every member of our community agrees. However, Amir has decided he would like the position for himself."

"So what?" Dan said. "He can't have it. Since Eli already has the backers, it's a non-issue."

"If only it were," Dad said. "Amir has been gathering support, and he plans to publicly challenge Eli."

"Publicly?" I said. "Who is he planning on doing this in front of? And when?"

"His plan is to turn all the local witch clans to his favor, and at their next celebration he will declare himself the leader of all seers," Dad replied.

"The next big date is Mabon?" I asked, and Tessa nodded.

"When's that?" Dan asked.

"Autumn equinox."

"That's over a month away," Dan said. "Which means, we have time to unravel whatever he's done."

"That's right we do," I said. "Where do we start?"

"Starting tomorrow, I will meet with the nearby clans," Dad said. "I've been told that Amir has resorted to threatening some of the clan elders."

"Jacob did say someone had threatened his life," I said.

"Jacob? Jacob Allwood?" Dad asked, and I nodded. "You're already on good terms with him?"

"I talk to him all the time," I said. "We've been besties ever since I found his murderer. It was his sister, Cecily, by the way."

Dad stilled. "Jacob's dead?"

"He is, but you'd never know it," I replied. "Once things came to a head with his sister I used the energy from the Allwood ancestors to power him up, so to speak. He's been as solid as the cats ever since," I finished, rubbing Pumpkin's ears for good measure.

Dad's gaze moved from me, to Pumpkin, and then to Tessa. "You're saying that you have the ability to make a spirit appear and behave as if they are a corporeal being."

"Yes. He can interact with anyone, seer, witch, or mortal."

"Where did you learn this? Who taught you?"

I shrugged. "No one. I just did it. We were trapped in the basement, Dan and me, and with us was Cecily and a bunch of goons she hired to beat us up, and our one and only ally was Jacob, but he was a spirit. There's a family cemetery on the property, so I asked the ancestors if I could use their energy and they agreed. They were also irritated with Cecily," I added.

Dad swallowed. "It's good that you've forged such a strong alliance with the Allwoods. That will help in my negotiations with the other clans."

"What about the Beauclaires?" Dan asked. Tessa shot him a glare. "Not you, Tess, the rest of them. Nathaniel Beauclaire has been hassling Eli for a long time. You'd think they'd want to do something about that embarrassment."

"Nathaniel is very, very powerful," Tessa said. "The current elders are children compared to him."

"Maybe they need new leadership."

"Perhaps they do, but that's beside the point," Dad said. "First, we must strengthen our alliances. Once that's done, we will deal with Amir."

"We've also got to protect Jada," I said. "She was possessed by Sarah Allwood for twenty years... and she's starting to remember some things."

"Things about Sarah?" Dad asked.

"I'm not sure," I said. "Jacob said she might share all of Sarah's memories."

"That's probably why Amir went to her," Tessa said. "He's seeking information about the Allwoods, and other clans."

"Do we think he's behind the bleeding hearts, too?" I asked.

Dad blinked. "There are bleeding hearts nearby?"

"They're all over town," I replied. "It's months past when they should be blooming, and it's way too hot. I'm worried they're a sign of something bigger."

Dad looked at Tessa, but she shook her head. "Eli is your daughter. You tell her."

"Tell me what?"

Dad raised his hand in the universal gesture for hang on a second. "Dan, Tessa, could you give us a moment?"

Tessa stood, and said, "Come along, Dan. We'll wait in the solarium."

"Okay." Dan followed Tess out of the kitchen, pausing to squeeze my shoulder on the way by. Once they were gone, I faced my father.

"What's so interesting about these bleeding hearts, and why can't Tessa talk about it?" I demanded.

"Tessa can talk about it. She's just... She's just being Tessa." Dad cleared his throat. "The bleeding hearts aren't a bad thing. In fact, for them to appear in multiple places you frequent is a very, very good thing."

"Does it have something to do with me becoming the Mistress of Seers?"

"No." Dad smoothed back my hair, and continued, "When bleeding hearts appear, it means that a seer has found love."

"Are you and Tessa getting back together?"

He laughed softly. "No. I hurt Tessa deeply, and I don't think she'll ever forgive me. These flowers are for you, and, I imagine, Dan."

"Love?" Of all the things I expected Dad to say, him telling me I'd found love wasn't one of them... but as I thought about Dan, our early morning calls and late-night movie marathons, I knew he was right. It felt right.

I looked toward the closed solarium door. "Both of us?"

"The flowers only appear if both parties feel the same way." Dad squeezed my hands. "Dan seems like a good man. I am very, very happy for you."

"I guess I'm happy for me too," I mumbled, still staring toward the solarium. "What does this mean?"

"It means whatever you want it to mean. Whether or not you wish to pursue a deeper relationship with him is up to you."

"And Dan, right? He has a say?"

"Based on how he looks at you, he's already made up his mind."

I thought about how Dan and I had stood in front of the windows as we talked about hosting baseball parties in the backyard, his arms around my waist as he kissed my neck… Then I remembered what we were looking at: The Ghost Guys nosing around the city lot. And on Dan's side of the fence was Charlotte's old greenhouse, which was packed with extremely poisonous plants.

"I know why the Ghost Guys are here," I said. "Dan's wife—"

"Wife?"

"She died," I said; I was so sick of explaining that. "I'm pretty sure she was possessed, or at least enchanted, for years, and it's what killed her. She built a poison garden in her back yard, and most of the plants are still in there, in her greenhouse."

"And you think this greenhouse is linked to Amir?"

"Amir and I first met when I was eighteen," I said, mentally sketching out a timeline. "That was almost eleven years ago. I remember how interested Amir was in our family. Dan married Charlotte—that was his wife's name—thirteen years ago, and she died seven years later. In that time she convinced Dan to move here, buy a house with a nice big yard, and help her set up her greenhouse."

"And Amir likes to play the long game." Dad rose from the table. "We need to tell the others."

Dad and I joined Tessa, Dan, and the cats in the solarium, and told them what we suspected about Amir and Charlotte. I watched Dan's face, and how it crumpled when I drew a line between Amir's plans and Charlotte. The bleeding hearts conversation would have to wait, probably for a long time.

"Bastard," Tessa muttered. "I never liked Amir."

"You're saying Charlotte married me because she was under some kind of a spell?" Dan asked.

"No. Maybe. I don't know." I blew out a breath; being told that your deceased yet still much-loved wife may have had ulterior motives behind marrying you can't be easy to hear. "When you first told me about her illness, and the symptoms her doctors didn't understand, I thought it sounded like possession. When another entity rides your body like that, your physical form crumbles."

"Jada's didn't," Dan pointed out.

"Jada had Nathaniel taking care of her," I said. "If the possession isn't consistent, it takes a long time for the host to... succumb," I finished, cringing as I said the word. "If she was only enchanted, it would take even longer." Dan outright scowled at that. Seeking to recover, I continued, "And then there's her greenhouse. Why did Charlotte have a poison garden?"

"Why do you?" Dan countered.

"I'm a seer! It's what we do!"

"Perhaps Tessa and I should check the yard," Dad said.

Tessa stood. "Excellent idea, Alex."

She and Dad left without another word. Once the door was shut behind them, I turned to Dan. "Why are you mad at me?"

Instead of answering my question, he asked, "When did you first think Charlotte was possessed?"

"When we were looking through the photo albums."

"Why didn't you say anything about it then?"

I threw up my hands. "I wasn't sure, I didn't want to upset you over nothing, and... And there's the fact that she's gone. I didn't want to tarnish her memory in your eyes."

"Yeah, well." Dan got up, and investigated a potted plant. "Can this kill me?"

"It's oregano, so theoretically, yes, but you'd need an awful lot. Or a really sharp oregano-wood stick."

"Are you saying Charlotte never loved me?"

"No. No!" I approached Dan and took his hands from the oregano, and ducked my head so I could see his eyes. "I am not saying that at all." When he still wouldn't look at me, I said. "Sit. We're going to find out exactly how Charlotte felt."

"How—wait, you can summon her?"

"Of course I can." I closed the curtains, but not before I saw my father and Tessa standing very, very close to each other in the rose garden. Interesting. "This way, you can gain some clarity. She probably will, too."

Once it was dark as it was going to get in the solarium on a summer's day, I sat next to Dan and took his hands. "Think about her. Help me call her."

"I try not to think about her, at least when I'm with you."

"It's okay." I rested my forehead against his. "I'm not the jealous type. What's your favorite memory of her?"

"At our wedding," he replied. "She was already sick, and the wedding almost didn't happen. Char's mother thought it would be too stressful, but Char insisted."

"Are you still close to her mother?"

"No. She passed a little while after Char did."

"I'm sorry." I adjusted our hands so Dan was in contact with my seer's mark. "Tell me the rest of your memory of her, at the wedding."

"It was when we cut the cake. Let me tell you, that cake was awful. It was dry, and the icing was hard as a rock and way too sweet. But Charlotte took a big bite and smiled, and said it was the best cake she ever had." A tear splashed onto my wrist. I didn't know if it was mine or Dan's. "Her eyes were big and wide and bright, and she looked so happy. I wish I could have kept her that happy."

"You did."

Dan's head snapped up. Sitting on the opposite chair was a slight, dark-haired woman with the large, expressive brown eyes. Even if I hadn't recognized her from the wedding pictures, I'd know that was Charlotte.

"Char, I—were you?" Dan asked. "Were you happy?"

"I was," she replied. "You always blamed yourself for me being sick, but it wasn't your fault. You did everything you could for me."

"If I'd done everything, you'd still be here."

Charlotte shook her head. "No, I wouldn't be, but you gave me many years of happiness. Thank you."

Dan stared at his dead wife's spirit, his eyes welling up. Since he needed a moment, I said, "Charlotte, my name is Eliza. Do you know what possession is?"

She nodded. "I do. I was possessed off and on for the last three years of my life."

"You were?" Dan demanded. "How?"

"I have no idea how, and I didn't know I was until after I died," Charlotte replied. "Remember when I put down my camera and took up gardening? Remember when I insisted we move, and that you had to build me that greenhouse, and all the exotic seed catalogs I ordered from?"

Dan nodded. "I remember all of it."

"That was when it started. And the funny part is that I didn't want to garden. I didn't want to tend all those toxic plants, nurture them only so they could kill. I hated it, but I couldn't stop or ask for help." Charlotte's gaze rested on the oleander. "I'd just started feeling better, had the audacity to hope I might live a long, happy life. Then I was compelled to grow those abominations, and they killed me."

"Which one killed you?" I asked.

"The castor bean," she replied. "I always knew it would. Once the greenhouse was a certain way along, I ate a handful of castor seeds, went up to bed, and let my spirit go."

"Were you compelled to eat the seeds?" I asked, momentarily sickened that Amir might have caused Charlotte's death.

"No. I did of my own free will." She reached toward Dan. "I'm sorry I couldn't hang on longer for you, but the possession kept my body going long after it should have given out. I was so, so tired."

"Don't apologize, not for anything," Dan said. "Did it hurt?"

Charlotte shook her head. "Ironically, it was the first time I felt alive."

"But you were sick before all of that," I said.

"Oh, yes," she replied. "I was a sick child with a weak heart, and grew into a sickly adult with many weaknesses. Most thought I wouldn't live to see twenty. I proved them wrong." She paused, then added, "Then I met Dan, and I felt better than I ever had in my life. Can love fortify a weak heart?"

"It can," I said. "When did your health go downhill again?"

"After our honeymoon. We didn't have one right after the wedding, for a variety of reasons."

"Then we won that trip," Dan said.

"Yes, the trip to England. I loved it, even when the tour took this odd detour and brought us to a poison garden. Of all things, a garden of poisons! But the grounds were lovely, and I took so many pictures. As soon as we got home, I started ordering seed catalogs, then I realized I couldn't grow on the scale I needed to in our condo, so I pressured Dan to buy a house. Of course, he did it."

"I'd do anything for you," Dan said.

Charlotte smiled at him. "You took very, very good care of me. I'll always love you, never forget that."

"I won't," Dan said, then Charlotte was gone.

"Where did she go?" Dan asked. "Bring her back!"

"She left on her own," I said. "Most spirits don't have enough energy to remain on the physical plan for very long. We can summon her again, after she's had some time to rest."

Dan stared at the empty chair. "I didn't get to tell her I love her."

"She knew." I wrapped my arms around Dan, and let him sob against my neck. "Believe me, she knew."

Chapter 21

Yard Stuff

It took Dan some time to compose himself after Charlotte left, and I didn't rush him. I couldn't imagine the emotional roller coaster he was riding, and I wouldn't have blamed him if he called it a day and went back to bed.

He didn't, though; whether he was being strong for himself or Charlotte, I didn't know. What I did know was that we sat together in the solarium for over an hour after Charlotte returned to the spirit plane. For that entire time, he refused to let go of my hand.

"Are Tessa and Alex still here?" he asked, eventually.

"They're in the garden," I replied. "You okay?"

"Yeah." He blew out a breath. "Actually, I'm a mess, but I've handled these feelings before. We're old friends."

"I'm sorry. I understand if you want to wash your hands of all of this."

"I don't think I can." Dan stared straight ahead at one of the hanging plants. "I will say that Charlotte cleared up my biggest fear."

"What were you afraid of?" Dan was the most fearless person I knew, and I'd grown up with Tessa.

"I worried that nothing I felt was my own experience," he replied. "What with Jada, and me getting possessed, and now everything with Charlotte... I worried that she and I had been manipulated into all of this. Now I know it started when we went to England. Charlotte married me because she wanted to, and that means a lot."

"In my line of work, motivations become cloudy more often than not," I said. "Now, do you see why it's important for me to know if I did things because I wanted to?"

"Yeah. I do." Dan faced me. "I'm sorry I doubted you. I get it now."

"I already forgave you. Let's get with Dad and Tess, see what our next steps are." I moved to rise, but he wouldn't stand or let go of my hand. "We do have to leave the solarium for that."

"Eli, I'm not good with words. I don't know if I can ever really express how much you mean to me, or thank you for everything you've given me."

I thought about all the bleeding hearts blooming away, and what Dad had told me about their significance. "I understand."

"Do you?"

"I do." I pulled him up next to me. "Come on. We've spoken with your lovely wife, and now we get to deal with my jerk of an ex."

We found Dad and Tessa sitting on one of the old benches in the rose garden. As we approached them, Dan's phone pinged. When he checked it, he frowned.

"I need to take this," he said, then he walked a few feet away. I looked at Dad and Tess, and shrugged.

"I guess it's a call from work," I said by way of an explanation.

"How are you two?" Tessa asked.

"Oh, we're great. I summoned his deceased wife to prove he hadn't been manipulated into all of these events, including but not limited to marrying said wife and moving to this town." I grinned like the Cheshire Cat. "And how are you?"

"Slightly better, I'd say," Dad said. "Did you talk to him about the flowers?"

"Not yet." I recalled something Jacob had said about Dan and me. "What does 'a circle unbroken' mean when you use that term to describe two people?"

"For seers? Nothing," Dad replied. "It's a witch term."

Tessa glanced at Dad and said, "It's what the mortals would call soulmates. It's when two partners replenish each other."

"As in, replenish energy?"

"Yes, it can be interpreted that way."

"Interesting."

"Lots of that going around," Dan said as he joined us. "That was the station," he said as he slid his phone into his back pocket. "First of all, Jada's complete file has disappeared from the hospital. I guess Bennet made good on his word and got the records."

"He is usually stealthier than that," Dad said.

"It might not have been Bennet," I said. "Jacob Allwood was also interested in Jada's file."

"I would expect more of Jacob, too," Dad said. "To claim an entire file arouses suspicion."

"Oh, it's aroused. The hospital is on lockdown and checking all surveillance footage. But what's more interesting," Dan continued, "is that Sanders, our forensics expert, tracked down Jada's family. They're out in Ohio now."

"Ohio," I scoffed. "Why would they go to that boring place?"

"After what they went through, they could probably use a dose of boring," Dan said. "It seems that when Jada was sixteen, she ended up with this boyfriend who appeared out of nowhere. Long story short, they swindled her family for everything—money, property, you name it. Jada was right; her family wants nothing to do with her. They even gave her a fake address when she reached out from the hospital so she wouldn't come by unexpectedly."

"Wow," I said. "Let me guess, this boyfriend was Nathanial Beauclaire masquerading as Nick Allwood?"

"Based on the description the parents gave of the boyfriend, I'd say so," Dan said. "Anyway, with the hospital on lockdown, Jada's safe, for now."

"Good, that's good," Dad said. "You say there's a poison garden on your property?"

"There is," Dan replied. "Apparently it's been there for some time, though I never knew what the plants were all about."

"May we visit it?" Dad asked. When Dan bristled, Dad added, "If we see what is growing there, we may be able to predict Amir's next move."

Dan glanced at me. I nodded slightly. "All right, let's go back to my place."

Dan drove all of us to his house, which was really our only option. My car was parked near my apartment, Tessa drove this ridiculous two-seater, and Dad didn't have a car, or a driver's license. As far as I knew, Dad had never driven anything with a motor a single day in his life, and he liked it that way.

When we got to Dan's, we skipped the house entirely and went straight to the backyard. The first thing we saw was a brand-new hole cut into the back fence. Dan drew his gun and advanced toward the fence.

"No one is on the property besides the four of us," Tessa said.

Dan glanced at her, then he lowered his gun. "Should I call this in, or do we have other ways of dealing with these people?"

"You should do what you think is best to protect your home," Dad replied. "While you consider your options, may we enter the greenhouse?"

"Go ahead. I'm going to check the house." Dan pointed to a glossy black camera mounted on the back of the house. "I've got video surveillance running, too. I'll download the footage."

"Are you going to send it to the station?" I asked.

"Let's see what's on it first." With that, Dan started walking around the perimeter of the house.

"Go with him," Tessa said.

"And do what? Hover?" I shook my head. "I'm more useful out here."

I walked past Dad and Tessa and opened the greenhouse. It looked exactly the same as it had a few days ago; long tables crowded with pots and other garden tools, along with some plants that were inexplicably still alive after years of neglect.

"I don't think anyone's been in here for the past few days," I said. "Nothing's been moved."

"Then why were Amir's men here," Dad murmured. "Are there any ritual items in the house?"

"No." I looked at the house, and hoped the Ghost Guys hadn't broken into Dan's home on a wild goose chase. "Maybe whatever they were looking for wasn't here."

"What's in there?" Tessa asked. She was pointing toward a small shed next to the stockade fence.

I shrugged. "I don't know."

We filed out of the greenhouse and approached the shed. I noticed that the lock was broken, but before I could say or do anything, Dan came outside carrying a tablet.

"Got the footage, and it has images of the perps," he announced.

"Is the house okay?"

"Yeah," he said, flashing me a smile. "They didn't get in. Check this out."

We crowded around the tablet as Dan pressed play. The backyard camera didn't capture the Ghost Guys making a hole in the fence, but it had recorded them wandering around the yard. They convened in front of the shed, then the leader, Mike, raised a phone to his ear.

Amir appeared on the screen a moment later.

"This our guy?" Dan asked.

"That's Amir Hassan," I confirmed. "How can he appear like that?"

"What's more, he disappeared. The four of them go into the shed, then they come out and fade away."

"He can move others that way, too?" Tessa asked. "If he's using time slips to move himself and others, that's far beyond the capabilities of the Amir we knew in Paris."

"Time slips are also forbidden," Dad added. "If the clans knew Amir was using them, they would likely rescind their support."

"Unless they wanted time slips to be un-forbidden," I muttered, then I remembered something. "When Amir re-opened that portal in Iran, why was that a bad thing?"

Realization lit Dad's eyes. "That portal leads to a temporal plane that mirrors our own. If one learns to navigate the plane, they can move through time on this plane."

"What's it look like inside this portal?" Dan asked. "Let me guess, it's all small stone rooms with dirt floors, and there's no light."

"That's correct," Dad said. "How did you know?"

"It's where Amir's been sending people," I said. "Now, we know who was behind the possessions."

Dan raised the tablet. "Since I have visuals, I'm calling it in. We need this super powered psycho caught." Dan turned to go back into the house, but I halted him with a hand on his arm.

"What's in the shed?" I asked.

"Yard stuff," he replied, then he looked toward the greenhouse, realization lighting in his eyes. "It's also where I put what's left of Charlotte's gardening things."

I pulled open the shed's doors. I was expecting to see a bunch of rakes and pruning shears. Instead, the interior of the shed was set up like an alchemist's lab.

Dan dropped the tablet. "What the hell."

CHAPTER 22

MADE FOR EACH OTHER

"THE LAST TIME I was in here, my lawn mower was just inside the door." Dan stood in the entrance of the shed, his gaze darting around the interior. "Where is my lawn mower?"

"There's a concealment charm on the door." Tessa ran her index finger down the doorjamb. "What's left of one, anyway. They broke it to gain entry."

"My shed has been concealing... this?" Dan gestured toward the long wooden table covered with bowls, flasks, and dried herbs in varying stages of preparedness. "And how come there's so much room in here?"

"The extra space is part of the spell," I said. "Whoever cast it created a portal from the shed's door to here. Wherever here is," I added.

Dan shook his head. "I just got that mower."

"Is this what Charlotte was creating with the herbs she grew?" Dad approached the worktable and picked up a few of the jars. "It appears that someone has been extracting plant essences. Distilling the poisons grown in the greenhouse, perhaps?"

Tessa investigated the bowls of herbs. "These leaves are nux vomica."

"What's that?" Dan asked.

"It's how you get strychnine," I replied. "But, there aren't any nux vomica trees in the greenhouse. Where did the leaves come from?"

"You can buy anything on the internet," Tessa said, then she opened a cabinet. Inside were stacks of notebooks. "This all looks like a very disorganized witch's still room." She opened one of the notebooks and flipped through the pages. "And the notebooks appear to be a nascent set of grimoires."

"Can you figure out what she was making?" I asked. "Then maybe we can make up an antidote. If there even is an antidote."

"All right. While you three work out what kind of witchcraft was happening in my shed under my nose, I'm putting out a BOLO on these creeps." With that, Dan stalked out of the shed and went inside the house.

"Crap." I winced as Dan banged the kitchen door shut. "I hope his head doesn't explode."

"Have a little faith," Tessa said. "Dan is strong, just like you." She picked up a stack of notebooks. "Alex, you grab the rest. We're going back to your place."

"We are?" Dad said. "But what if Eli needs us?"

"Eli will be fine." Tessa winked at me, and I remembered her car was at Gran's.

"I can ask Dan to drive you back," I began, but Tessa shook her head.

"It's not too far to walk. Come along, Alex."

Dad picked up a stack of notebooks, said a quick goodbye to me, and followed Tessa out of the shed. I had a last look around the interior, noting the varied items, then I stepped outside the shed and shut the door. I saw Dan through the kitchen window, then I went to join him inside the house.

And realized I was alone with Dan.

I bit the inside of my cheek and stepped into the kitchen. Dan was staring out the back window at the hole in the fence, his hands braced on the counter. He looked exhausted, and now that I thought about it, I was pretty tired, too.

"Hey."

Dan glanced over his shoulder, then he turned around and faced me. "Hey. What did you find out there?"

"Nothing else, at least not yet. Dad and Tessa took the notebooks back to Gran's. They're going to look through them, see what they can find." I noted the golden rays from the sun slanting across the tile floor. "It's been a hell of a day."

"It sure has. I don't know if I've ever been to so many places as we've hit up over the past two days, and I used to be a beat cop."

"You were?"

"Yeah, back in New York."

I was struck by how much I didn't know about Dan. "Are you from New York?"

"Queens. I lived there all my life, never thought I'd leave... Then, we came here." Dan cast a longing glance toward the backyard, and Charlotte's greenhouse. "Now, it's just me."

And me, the outsider who keeps wrecking things.

"I-I should go," I said. "You look beat, and I know I am, and—"

"You don't have to go."

"Like you said, we've been at this all day, and yesterday, and now they've been in your yard and your shed, and... And I'm sorry. I keep screwing up your life, and I don't want to do that anymore."

I turned to go, then Dan said, "Did it ever occur to you that my life was already pretty screwed up, and you're the one fixing it?"

I stopped moving, but I didn't look at him. "It doesn't seem that way."

Dan stood in front of me and took my hands. "You told Charlotte love can fortify a weak heart. As much as I did that for Char, I think you did that for me."

"Were you sick?"

"Not physically, but I was miserable. Depression, anxiety... I had it all, got diagnosed with everything, and everyone kept telling me it would be fine. To be expected, they'd say, because I lost my wife so young. You'll be fine, they'd say. But I wasn't. I got worse and worse... And then there was one day at work, when I had to take a statement on this weird ass case."

"How weird?"

"Incredibly weird, and I was beyond pissed that I had to do it. But I was on thin ice with the chief already, and when he told me to do it, I decided to suck it up for once and get it over with."

"Why were you on thin ice?"

"That is a story for another time. Anyway, this case was strange, like bad science fiction movie strange. Someone was poisoning retirees with these black berries, and the PI that cracked the case was coming in to make her statement."

I felt my face warm. "I can't believe you remember that."

"How could I forget the day the most beautiful woman I've ever seen walked into the place where I work?" I tried hiding my face against his chest, but Dan tilted up my chin. "Everything changed after that. You pulled me out of my funk."

"I didn't even do anything."

"You did. I don't know how, but you did. Maybe I just needed to meet you." He gathered me closer and we held each other, my head tucked underneath his chin. "However it happened, it happened."

"I'm glad. Really." I pulled away, ignoring how cold I felt without him. "I'll let you get some rest."

I'd only taken three steps when Dan said, "In the solarium, before you and Alex joined us. Tessa told me what the flowers mean."

I almost kept walking. "Why did she do that?"

"Because I asked her."

"And what did you think after she told you?"

"That I love you, too."

I couldn't move. I could barely breathe. I was terrified that if I moved or spoke, everything would shatter around me; Dan would be possessed again, it was Amir in disguise, it was all a cruel joke.

Nothing good lasts, at least not for me. But this was good. Dan and I were good together.

Shouldn't I at least try?

Dan touched my shoulder. When I didn't run off, he came closer, the length of his body against my back. He moved my hair to the side and pressed his cheek against my neck. "You're always so warm here."

"You can't... you don't know me."

"Don't I? What I do know is that I'm having the strangest day of my life. I talked to my dead wife, and that wasn't even the strangest part. Magicians broke into my shed, then they disappeared and left behind a wizard's craft room." He slid his arms around my waist, and continued, "And I know that I wouldn't want to deal with these strange and weird things with anyone but you."

I clutched his forearms, my own crossed over my stomach, and said, "I guess I don't mind the weird so much with you, either."

"See that? We were made for each other."

Chapter 23

A Whole Town Full Of Flowers

"We should go back to your apartment."

I leaned back and regarded Dan. We were still standing in the kitchen, holding each other, though I had turned around for a proper embrace. "You were just complaining about all the places we've been to, and you want to go to another one?"

"I was not complaining. Just stating facts." He kissed the top of my head, then he pulled away and picked up his tablet. "However, if Amir and the rest come back, I think it'll be better if we're not here. I'm not equipped for magical combat."

"Are you sure the house will be safe?"

"The surveillance is up and running, and I can check it remotely. Once I lock up, we should be good to go." He looked up, frowning. "Unless you don't want me to go to your place with you. I can drive you home and come back here."

He was so stinking cute when he was flustered. "It's fine. Do you want to pack anything?"

"Pack. Um. Yeah." Dan set down his tablet and went off to pack whatever boys bring to sleepovers. I looked down at myself; after all the running around we'd done, I was dying for a shower. Add to that my sore feet, and my stomach, which hadn't had anything in it since breakfast, and I was ready to call it a night.

When Dan returned to the kitchen with a backpack slung over his shoulder, I was watering the potted herbs over the kitchen sink with a measuring cup I found in the pantry. "Do you ever cook with these?"

"I meant to. Maybe I'll start tomorrow."

I set the cup in the sink. "I'm ready if you are."

And we were off. The drive to my apartment was short, and silent, and as awkward as showing up late to a test you hadn't studied for. Usually, when I felt confused or nervous, my go-to response was babbling like the proverbial brook, but I couldn't figure out why I was so anxious. Dan had been to my place dozens of times. Him coming over wasn't anything new or out of the ordinary. I glanced at Dan's bag where it sat on the back seat, and understood.

Dan was going to stay the night, on purpose this time.

I'd never brought a date back to my apartment. Truth be told, I'd been on very few dates since I broke things off with Amir; our relationship had been exciting, and tumultuous, and the end had been like a roller coaster crashing into a freight train. It had been such an epic disaster I'd sworn off all relationships, and seriously considered becoming a nun.

Every date I'd been on since my and Amir's demise had been a continuation of the disaster in one form or another; either they weren't my type, or they were only interested in me because of my paranormal abilities, or—as in the case of Nathaniel Beauclaire masquerading as Nick Allwood—they were my enemies in disguise. But Dan wasn't like any of those past partners, or potential partners. He understood me in a way others never did, and didn't expect me to change to fit any of society's preconceived ideals. He wanted me, for me.

I touched Dan's hand where it rested on the gearshift. He turned it over and laced his fingers with mine, then he brought our hands to his mouth and kissed my knuckles.

"A few years ago, I wanted to become a nun."

"Glad you didn't go through with that. Want to stop for something to eat?"

"If you want. I have food at home."

"What, cereal and bananas?"

"The two best foods."

Dan found a parking spot near my building, and we climbed the stairs to my apartment. My hands trembled as I unlocked the door, then I took a deep breath and pushed it open.

"We're here," I announced, rather needlessly. "I'm going to change."

"Okay." Dan set his bag on the floor next to the door and went into the kitchen. Since he was occupied, I went into my bedroom, pulling my shirt up and over my head as I walked. I tossed it into the laundry basket, then I opened my closet and rooted around for something comfortable.

"Your bananas are black," Dan yelled from the kitchen.

"They are not."

"You can't even use these for banana bread."

"I don't like banana bread, so who cares?" I yelled back, then I unhooked my bra and slid it off my arms.

"I'm going to order something," Dan said. "I'm starving, and you must be, too."

"All right. Menus are in the drawer."

"They're where?" Dan asked, and I realized he was standing in the bedroom doorway. I turned around and saw him staring at me like a deer in headlights.

"In the drawer next to the fridge." I dropped my bra into the laundry basket and stood there, only topless though I felt completely bare. I'm not body shy. Most members of the supernatural community are fine with nudity; when you grow up in and around rituals that involve varying degrees of undress, you got over it pretty quickly. But Dan hadn't grown up like me.

Dan would turn around if I asked him to. Hell, he would go back home and never mention this again, if he thought that was what I wanted. Did I want him to leave?

I bit my lip. I was unsure about so many things, but I was certain about one thing.

I wanted him to stay, right here with me.

"You should take your shirt off," I said, my voice hardly wavering. "So we match."

He did. I raked my gaze across his upper body, from his broad shoulders to the trail of dark hair that disappeared beneath his belt.

I kicked off my shoes and unbuttoned my jeans, and that was the signal Dan needed. He crossed the room in two steps, then he tilted my chin up and kissed me. The tips of my breasts grazed his chest and set every nerve in my body on fire. I wrapped my arms around Dan's neck as his big, calloused hands glided down my back and cupped my butt.

I set my hand on his chest. "Wait."

Dan's hands moved away from my butt lightning fast. "Eli, I wouldn't have—"

"It's okay," I said over him. "I just need to do something. One sec."

I ran out of the bedroom, grabbed my bag, and returned to a bewildered Dan standing in the middle of the room. I found the anti-possession oil I'd made with Jacob, uncorked the bottle, and anointed Dan's forehead.

"What's your name?" I asked.

"Dan. Daniel Edward Lyons."

"Do you have any other names?"

"No."

"Oh, thank god," I said, slumping against him. "If you'd been possessed again, I think it would have killed me."

Dan took the bottle from my hands and set it aside. "You were really worried about that?"

"When we were together before, and then it turned out not to be you, I was devastated." I laid my cheek against his chest as his arms came around my shoulders. "If it happened that way again, I don't know what I'd do."

"You want to be with me that badly?"

"Yeah." I squeezed my eyes shut, and continued. "I'm not good with words, either."

"It's okay. There's a whole town full of flowers out there telling me how you feel."

I laughed against his chest. "I guess there are." I peeked up at him. "I killed the moment, huh?"

Dan responded by sliding his hands back down to my thighs and lifting me against him, then he turned around and dropped me onto the bed. I lost my breath, then his mouth was on mine and I forgot about breathing altogether. His hands roamed over my body as Dan kissed a path from my mouth down my throat, then he took one of my breasts in his mouth while his hand cupped the other. He pinched my nipple, and I squealed.

"Was that a good noise?"

"Good," I replied, threading my fingers into his hair. "Very good."

His fingers glided down past my navel. Dan mumbled something as he kissed my throat, then his hand slid inside my jeans and touched me. It wasn't anything like when we'd been in the shower, when the spirit possessing him had been on a mission to make me come. Dan's—real Dan's—touch was soft, and gentle. He was so tender it brought tears to my eyes.

"Is it okay if I take these off?" he asked.

"You first."

He stood beside the bed, never breaking eye contact with me as he unfastened his belt and shed the rest of his clothes. I remembered exactly what his body looked like, but I still sucked in a breath when his cock sprang free from his pants, hard and tall and maybe a bit intimidating. Maybe a lot intimidating.

Once he was naked, Dan tugged my clothes off my hips and down my legs, then he laid his body on top of mine. "You're beautiful, you know that?"

"Only when you're looking at me."

"Well, I look at you all the time," he began, then he laughed awkwardly and ducked his head. "I don't know why I'm so nervous."

"I am, too." I wrapped one of my legs around his hip. "Want to be nervous together?"

Dan chuckled, then he slid a hand underneath my thigh and aligned himself against me. "Tell me what you want."

I reached between us and took the length of him in my hand. "I want you."

Dan positioned his cock against me as I linked my ankles behind his back, then he pushed himself into me. I wasn't as ready as I'd thought and it was not comfortable, but I didn't want him to stop.

Dan moved, and my whole body shuddered. "You okay?"

"Yeah." Even my voice was shaky. "I'm just getting used to you."

He grunted, then he withdrew and moved down my body so quickly I didn't have time to ask what he was doing. A moment later his mouth was on me, kissing and licking and holy hell I couldn't even think straight. My hips bucked as sensations overloaded me, but Dan held me down and wrung the most mind-splittingly intense orgasm I'd ever had out of my body. He kissed his way up my body as I floated back to earth, and slid his cock back inside me.

"That's better," he said, his hips finding their rhythm as he thrust into me. "You with me, babe?"

I mumbled an affirmation, then Dan pressed his forehead against mine and drove himself into me until I saw stars. As I came a second time, he shuddered and had his release, then he dropped onto the mattress beside me, spent.

"That was amazing," I said, panting. "So glad I'm not a nun."

He kissed me between my breasts, right over my heart. "Me, too."

"Come back to bed!"

"In a minute."

I rolled over and punched my pillow into shape. It was hours later than I usually got out of bed, and I didn't care. It was Sunday, I had no clients booked, and I'd just had one of the best nights of my life. Despite our exhaustion, Dan and I had hardly slept. Instead, we talked, and kissed, and ordered pizza, and watched a ton of cheesy movies. It had been perfect.

"Here I am," he announced, striding into the room. He'd only just gotten to the bed when his phone pinged. "It's work," he said, then he accepted the call.

"Lyons. What? When?" Dan left the room and returned with his bag. "I can be there in fifteen."

"What happened?" I asked.

Dan tossed the phone onto the bed. "Jada's missing."

CHAPTER 24

LINEAGE

DAN AND I THREW on some clothes and ran down the stairs toward his car. We didn't know how or why Jada had disappeared, but I was certain nothing good would come of it. When I got outside, I stopped dead in my tracks.

Bleeding hearts lined both sides of the road.

"Holy shit," I mumbled, as Dan bumped into my back.

"Why'd you stop?" he asked, then he saw the ocean of pink flowers and sucked in a breath. "Are those for us?"

"Um, I guess?" I looked up at him. "I did not know this would happen."

"Never a dull moment, is there? Come on, they're waiting for me at the hospital."

We got in the car and sped toward the hospital. "I'm going to call Tessa and tell her what happened."

"You two really are close," he began, then he asked, "Oh, you mean about Jada?"

"Despite what the media portrays, women have other things to talk about than boys," I said, and placed the call. Tessa picked up on the first ring.

"The front, back, *and side yards* are packed with bleeding hearts," she said. "Either you had the best sex of your life, or we're dealing with a botanist with a vendetta."

I have got to find a way to counteract these stupid flowers. "Ignore the flowers. Jada's gone missing."

"I thought the hospital was on lockdown," she said.

"So did we. So did everyone." Dan screeched into the hospital's parking lot. "This supposed lockdown happened after someone took her file."

"I know what you're thinking. I'll reach out to Bennet."

"Thanks, Tess. Tell Dad I'll call soon."

I ended the call as Dan parked near the front of the hospital. He jumped out of the car and made a beeline for the rest of the police, but I hung back. For one, I wasn't a cop, and didn't want to intrude where I didn't belong. I also wanted to find out what the hospital itself would tell me about Jada's disappearance.

I couldn't always pick up information from physical locations, but I was successful more often than not. As I stared at the hospital's façade, I saw some place safe and secure, that was staffed by some of the best medical professionals in the state. I also saw several armed security guards, which made me wonder how Jada got out without being spotted, or shot.

I wondered if she had been taken against her will.

"Miss Moore."

I turned toward the voice and saw Nathaniel Beauclaire standing alongside the parking lot, hiding in the shrubbery. "You've got some nerve," I began.

"Do you know where Jada is?" he demanded.

"You don't have her?"

"No," he said, panicked. "I came for my daily visit with her, and she was gone!"

"You were visiting her every day? But you're not on the approved visitor list."

"I come to her in her dreams. It's easy enough, but you need to know where and when your subject sleeps. When I couldn't make contact with her this morning, I infiltrated the hospital and found her gone."

"You infiltrated," I said, then I realized if he knew how to get in, he knew how to get out. "How could she have left without raising an alarm?"

"That's just it. I don't know." Nathaniel looked up at the windows on the upper floors. "Her room is locked every night and not reopened until the morning nurse arrives at nine. The windows don't open, and the vents are too small to crawl through. I will say this, however she left, she didn't do it alone."

That meant someone with magical abilities—probably a witch—had gotten Jada out. "This is bad for you, isn't it?" I asked. "Jada knows a lot about you and Sarah. And Jemima, too, I'd wager."

Nathaniel narrowed his eyes. "I see you've been asking some rather pointed questions. Let me give you one of the answers you seek, as a show of my good faith. Sarah is no longer on your list of enemies."

"You finally offed her, once and for all?"

"No. You did."

I paused, caught off guard by his admission. "You mean, when I exorcised her from Jada, that was the end of her?"

"Not only that. Her remains were being cared for at the orchard." My confusion must have been plain on my face, because Nathaniel rolled his eyes. "Surely you understand that making the proper offerings to a witch's mortal remains is the key to keeping their spirit strong?"

"Sarah was the skeleton in the cider vat," I said, and he nodded. "I heard all the fruit in the orchard was rotting away."

"It is, because Sarah's spirit no longer feeds it."

"It must feel great to be finally rid of her. What does this mean for Jemima?"

"It means I can finally get her back." Nathaniel tilted his head back, again gazing toward Jada's window. "It means I need Jada now, more than ever."

"I'm not going to help you find Jada just so you can stick your wife's spirit in her, like you tried to do to me," I said. "You're sick."

"I need Sarah's knowledge in order to retrieve Jemima, and Jada has it," Nathaniel said, thus confirming that Jada had all of Sarah's memories locked inside her mind. "We need to find Jada. "

"We do," I said, not pleased about being in agreement with my mortal enemy. "She might be scared, and alone."

"Our reasons differ, but we have the same goal," Nathaniel said. "We should work together."

"You've almost killed me how many times?" I demanded. "And how many other people are dead because of you and your insane family?"

Nathaniel shrugged. "I am not suggesting we become allies, merely that we set our differences aside until this is resolved. And do not forget, Miss Moore, not so long ago you enjoyed my attentions."

The memory of me and Nathaniel—who at the time was pretending to be Nick Allwood—making out on my waiting room couch flashed behind my eyes... and that brought up another question. "Did you have Dan possessed?"

Nathaniel blinked. "Your mortal? No. Why would I?'

The way he was taken aback by my question, coupled with his frank denial, made me believe him. "Someone did."

Nathaniel looked past me. "Is he possessed now?"

"I certainly hope not."

I watched Dan as he spoke with the other police officers, nodding as they filled him in on the situation. He looked up and his gaze found me, and he smiled.

Then he saw Nathaniel.

"You should go," I said to Nathaniel.

"That mortal can't harm me."

Dan was stalking toward us, his hand hovering over his gun. "That kind of arrogance gets witches killed."

"Get away from Eli," Dan said when he was close enough. "Where's Jada?"

"Damned if I know," Nathaniel said.

"He doesn't have her."

Dan glanced at me. "You believe him?"

"It's in his best interests to know where Jada is," I replied. "It seems like Nathaniel might need our help."

Dan drew me aside. "You want to work with this guy?"

"I want to find Jada." I turned to Nathaniel. "If we work together, it's to find Jada. Nothing more."

"Agreed," Nathaniel said.

"But," I continued, "first I have a few questions."

Nathaniel rolled his eyes again. "Of course you do. Please, ask away."

"You already said you didn't possess Dan," I began. "Do you know who did?"

"I do not."

"Why did you leave a buckle at Dim Sum Delight?"

"Let me respond to your inquiry with a question of my own. What is Dim Sum Delight?"

"We tracked you there, and you left a buckle..." Nathaniel's blank face explained everything. He had no idea what I was talking about.

"If you didn't leave the buckle, who did?" I asked.

"I've no idea," Nathaniel said. "If you have this item, I can try to recognize the magical signature."

"We gave it to—" I gasped.

"Bennet," Dan finished. "Who also may have taken Jada's file."

"Someone must be controlling him," I said, unwilling to believe Bennet would betray us on his own.

"Think it's Amir?" Dan asked.

"Amir Hassan?" Nathaniel said. "Are you spending time with that fool again? Miss Moore, your love life is most inconvenient, isn't it?"

"How do you even know I used to date Amir?" I demanded. "It happened in a whole different country."

Nathaniel shrugged. "I like to be well informed."

I glared at Nathaniel. "Stay here, and watch for clues. Dan and I have someplace to be."

We walked away from Nathaniel. "Where to?" Dan asked.

"Let's get to Bennet before this gets any worse."

Eli: Guess what? That buckle from the restaurant wasn't from Nathaniel.

Eli: I bet Amir left it for us.

Tessa: Wonderful. Bennet's not at home.

Eli: We'll check the school.

Tessa: On our way.

Dan drove from the hospital to the college like a bat out of hell. I didn't ask him to slow down, or be more cautious. I just held on, and hoped I was wrong about Bennet being under Amir's influence. My gut told me I was spot on.

As we sped across town, I couldn't help but notice the plethora of bleeding hearts that lined the road, springing up from every available patch of dirt. "This is embarrassing."

"What? The flowers?" Dan glanced at me—which was terrifying, based on how fast he was driving—and flashed me a self-satisfied grin. "Think they're all because of last night? Impressive, huh?"

"Eyes on the road, Lyons."

Being that it was Sunday, the college's parking lot was empty. Dan ignored the marked travel lanes and drove straight toward Bennet's building, and parked on the sidewalk right in front of the main door.

"What if he's not here?" I asked as we exited the car.

"If he's not, we'll keep looking until we find him," Dan said. I heard another car, and saw Tessa pull into the lot. "Come on," Dan said. "They know where we're headed."

We ran up the stairs to Bennet's office. The doors from the stairwell to the corridor were locked. Without a word I dropped to my knees and withdrew my lock picks.

"Move aside," Tessa said as she cleared the top of the stairs. I scrambled out of the way as Tessa pointed at the door. Sparks exploded from the lock and the doors flew open. Tessa strode inside Bennet's office without missing a beat.

"Bennet," she yelled. "You will explain your actions, and explain them now."

"Explain what, exactly?" Bennet asked as he appeared from behind a bookcase. "You could have knocked, Isabella. I would have admitted you soon enough."

"Do not call me Isabella," Tessa seethed. "What have you done?"

"This morning? I've had tea, done some reading, and am planning on a spot of research. Why? Have you need of something?"

Tessa raised her hand as if to throw a punch. I grabbed her arm and said, "He's not himself! Bennet's never intentionally obtuse. We need to find that buckle."

"What am I looking for?" Dan demanded. "Describe."

"It's an old-fashioned metal buckle, like one from a Pilgrim hat," I said, then my father entered the office. "Hey, Dad."

"I was setting wards," Dad said. "We don't need anyone disturbing us."

"About that," I began. "Nathaniel Beauclaire didn't take Jada."

Dad stopped walking. "Amir?"

"Seems likely." Dad nodded, then he resumed walking toward a wall of file cabinets. "What are you looking for?"

"When we got to Bennet's home, I checked the records room. The lineages are gone."

"The witch lineages?"

"No." Dad yanked open the top cabinet. "Seer."

"Oh. Why would anyone want those?" Seer lineage in general wasn't that interesting. The only local seers were Dad and me, and our relationship was rather straightforward.

"Someone could use them against you." Before I could ask exactly how information everyone already knew could be harmful, I heard Dan and Tessa arguing.

"You're gonna kill him," Dan said. I returned to the front of the office and found Bennet in his chair while Dan and Tess stood over him. Nothing was touching Bennet, but his body and limbs looked as if they were being pummeled by gale force winds.

"She won't," I said; I'd watched Tessa restrain people in such a manner before. "We need Bennet out of the way while we search for the buckle."

Tessa nodded. "It's on him, somewhere."

Dan pursed his lips. "All right, I've frisked plenty of people. Tess, can you let him stand?" Tessa flicked her wrist and Bennet rose into the air like a marionette without strings. Dan swallowed, then he started searching Bennet.

"It's his belt buckle," I said when Dan lifted Bennet's waistcoat.

"Little on the nose," Dan muttered as he unfastened Bennet's belt and pulled it free. Dan flung the belt aside as if it was a cobra poised to strike.

"Bennet?" I stepped closer and peered at him. His eyes were bleary behind his glasses, and beads of sweat formed on his forehead. "Are you okay?"

"Eliza?" He focused on me, then gasped. "Gods, Eliza, what have I done?"

Tessa lowered him into his chair. "None of it was your fault." She found his handkerchief in his chest pocket and dabbed at his brow. "We were all duped, Bennet."

"Duped into doing what?" I asked. When no one answered me, I picked up Bennet's belt and examined the buckle. It was covered in a familiar, gritty slime.

"Same blue residue as my witchfinder." I set the buckle on Bennet's desk. "Looks like confirmation that Amir was responsible for the chaos at the restaurant, too."

"I thought you said his magic was orange," Dan said to Tessa. "This is the same blue as before."

She shrugged. "His motivations must have changed."

"Why does Amir want the seer lineage records?" I asked. "What would they even do for him?"

Bennet's eyes widened, and he glanced at Tessa. She shook her head slightly, and said, "Alex is checking the records now."

"Alexander is here?" Bennet said.

"I am," Dad said, striding into the office. "Bug, we need to talk."

"Great. Let's talk."

"Alone would be better."

"Why? More than half of the people in this room already know whatever you're going to tell me." I crossed my arms over my chest. "Well?"

Dad took a deep breath, and said, "Your mother was a witch."

CHAPTER 25

EVERYTHING'S OUT IN THE LIGHT

I FELT LIKE THE floor had fallen out from under me. "What?"

"I didn't know she was a witch, not at first," Dad continued. "She didn't even know. Christina was born in an orphanage, and had no knowledge of her family."

"When did you know?" Dan prompted, when shock kept me silent.

"Not until she was pregnant," Dad replied. "As Eli grew, Christina's innate magic manifested. At first they were small things, like the weather altering itself to ensure she wasn't too warm or cold."

"Altering the weather is not a small thing," I said.

Dad smiled sadly. "No, it is not. Neither were the flowers that sprung up wherever she walked, or the clouds of butterflies that would swarm her in the garden. Eventually Ma had enough and did some investigating of her own."

"Gran went to The Open Arms Center and spoke to Marion?" I ventured.

Dad blinked. "Yes. How did you know?"

"Dan and I met Marion. A few days ago, actually." I scrubbed my face with my hands. "If Mom was a witch, why did she freak out and abandon me when my powers manifested?"

"Christina wanted nothing to do with magic," Dad replied. "She made me promise to let you grow up as a mortal—or as a normal person, as she put it—until your sixteenth birthday. That was to be when I told you the truth, and... and you know what happened."

"No, I don't," I said. "I know she left me. That's it. I was alone in a hospital room for a week before Gran came for me. What else happened?"

"Perhaps I can offer some enlightenment," Bennet said. "Your grandmother—Helena—wanted documents drawn up, giving her parental rights in place of your mother. It's a tricky thing discharging a minor from a hospital when you are not their legal guardian, and being that your other parent was away," Bennet nodded toward Dad, "Helena wanted to ensure that when she brought you home, you would stay with her. She didn't feel it was right for your mother to walk out in and out of your life whenever it was convenient for her."

"You created these documents?" I asked.

"Oh, no. I assisted Helena, but we went through all the proper legal channels. That's why it took a week before she could retrieve you."

"You weren't supposed to be alone for so long," Dad added. "My intent was to take full custody of you immediately, but my journey home was delayed."

As your journeys often are. "Did she ever try to get me back? Did she ever write, or call?"

Dad shook his head. "I'm sorry, Bug. I don't know what became of your mother after she left you at the hospital. Neither I nor Ma ever heard from her again."

I stared at Dad, then Bennet, and finally Tessa. "Did you know, too?"

"I didn't, until Alex told me earlier today," she replied. "I only ever saw Christina twice. I knew nothing about her, except that she was having you."

I nodded. At least Tessa hadn't betrayed me. "Explain how my mother being a witch can work in Amir's favor."

Bennet hung his head. "He intends to prove that your lineage makes you unfit to serve as the seers' leader, and take the position for himself."

Laughter bubbled up from my throat. "I never wanted to do this, anyway. He can have it," I said, then I turned around and left Bennet's office. I'd only meant to step outside and get some air, but my feet wouldn't stop moving. I descended the stairs and pushed my way out of the building and into the blinding sun. An old saying came to mind: everything done in the dark will eventually come into the light.

I sure wasn't in the dark now.

I heard the double doors open and clang shut, then Dan stood beside me. "Are you sure you want to do this?" I asked.

"Stand here?"

"Be with me." I shut my eyes and turned my face skyward. "My life is a mess. I am a mess, and now I can either let Amir take a position I never wanted, or I can fight to stay something I don't want to be."

"Are those your only options?"

"Yes. No. I don't know." I rolled my neck from shoulder to shoulder; once upon a time, I'd taken a dance class, and the instructor told us that flexing our neck muscles would help settle our thoughts. It never worked, at least not for me. "What else can I do?"

"What do you want to do?" Dan asked.

"I want to go home, and go back to bed."

"I'm down for that." Dan draped his arm around my shoulder, and I turned into him. Why had I resisted him for so long? Being in his arms didn't make anything better, but it made me feel like it could be better. I felt like I could handle Amir, and the issue of heritage, and anything else that life decided to throw at me.

At us. Dan and I were an us. Maybe this sense of completeness is what Jacob meant when he called us a circle unbroken.

I recalled what Marion said about Cecily Allwood's interest in the baby that became my mother. What if Jacob and I were related?

"What will happen if Amir takes over?" Dan asked. "Will he hurt people?"

"Yeah. Maybe not intentionally, but Amir takes what he wants. If people get in his way, he removes or eliminates them."

"Seems like you're the one in his way."

"He's only doing this because he thinks I'm weak. Gran was strong, and no one questioned her. He thinks I'm a stupid kid."

Dan held my face in his hands. "You're not a kid, and you're sure as hell not stupid. You're brilliant, and strong, and you have so much knowledge and power packed inside you. He's nothing compared to you."

"Really?"

"You know I always say what I mean." Dan smiled to himself. "I have an idea about all of this, if you're willing to hear one."

"Tell me."

"What if instead of approaching this as you fighting to keep a job, we fight to show the world how bad Amir really is?"

I kissed him, full on the lips. "Who's the brilliant one now?

Chapter 26

Power

"It's a sound idea," Dad said, after we told him, Tessa, and Bennet that we wanted to disgrace Amir, and therefore prove that I was the better option for leading the seer community. "How will we go about this?"

"I am up for suggestions," I said. "Is there any documented evidence of Amir behaving badly?"

"I have the video surveillance of him using that time spell in my yard," Dan said. "We've also got a sworn statement from the cook at the Chinese restaurant."

"That's all well and good, but those are all mortal sources," Bennet said. "What we need are accusations made toward him by members of the supernatural community. Alexander, have there been any allegations of wrongdoing brought against Amir by any witches, or seers?"

"Not that I'm aware of," Dad replied. "There's been plenty of hearsay over the years, but as far as I know, there haven't been any formal charges levied at him since that incident in Persia."

"And he has proof that I'm not a real seer," I muttered.

"You are a seer," Dad said. "Your abilities prove it more than my words ever could. If anything, your mother's influence makes you more powerful."

"If that's the case, why does Amir think he can use Eli's mother against her?" Dan asked.

"Those born from magic tend to be very old-fashioned," Tessa said. "Most eschew all aspects of modern life, refusing to have basic technology such as a landline telephone or even a radio. Alex doesn't even know how to drive."

"I understand the concept," Dad said. "I just don't see it as necessary."

"They you can walk home," she said, with a pat to Dad's arm. "Ironically, Jacob Allwood was one of the few witches to embrace technology, and look at what happened to him."

"He's doing great now," Dan said. "You'd never know he was dead."

Dad glanced at Tessa. She turned toward Bennet, who looked away. "Why is Jacob being a robust spirit a bad thing?" I asked.

Dad gestured for Bennet to explain. "One of the reason we keep the lineages is to ensure no witch and seer have issue, which then rises to a position of power," he began. "If you study witchcraft along with the principals of death, you could become quite powerful. Perhaps too powerful."

"But Gran was powerful," I said. "She could do amazing things, and no one batted an eye."

"No one batted an eye when you were around," Dad said. "Ma fought for her position, and she fought to keep it. She was strong, but more than that, she was stubborn. She felt that being the Matriarch was her right, and she wouldn't let anyone take that from her."

"Then, isn't it Eli's right to lead?" Dan asked. "Or yours?"

We all looked at Bennet. "I suppose it depends on how you look at it. The Moores have overseen all seers on this continent for centuries, but in the old country, things were handled differently."

"Which old country are we talking about?" Dan asked.

"England, of course," Bennet replied. "There, each clan would submit the name of their strongest member, and the names would go into a lottery. Whoever won the draw became the new leader."

"And Amir's British," Dan said. "So, he wants to go back to the good old days. How often was a new leader selected?"

"As often as needed, usually upon the death or incapacitation of the prior leader."

Dan nodded. "Incapacitation. That sounds awful."

"Usually, it was."

"The Allwoods are still the strongest clan in the area, correct?" I asked; if I had to hear another one of Bennet's moldy old facts, I was going to scream. "Maybe we're looking at this the wrong way. Maybe instead of discrediting Amir, what I really need is witch support."

"We know Jacob's on your side," Dan said. "How many more clans have we got?"

"Historically, this region has been dominated by six clans," Bennet replied. "In addition to the Allwoods, there are the Howe, Wardwell, Burroughs, and Martin families."

"That's five clans," Dan said. "Who's number six?"

"Beauclaire," Tessa replied. "Though there's hardly any of us left, and I'm not supposed to associate with them."

"If not you, then who leads the Beauclaires?" Dan asked. "That Nathaniel piece of crap?"

"Technically, yes, since he is older than I am," Tess replied.

"It doesn't matter," I said. "Nathaniel needs us to get Jada back. If he's in charge, he'll back me. Not that I don't prefer you," I said to Tessa.

"Love you, too, Eli."

"Do you trust Nathaniel?" Dad asked.

"Not for a hot second, but he's used me plenty. It's time I used him for a change," I said. "If the Allwoods and Beauclaires are with me, that's a third of the families. I just need one more on my side, and Amir won't have a majority."

"It's not a democracy," Bennet said. "Witches are about power, not numbers."

Tessa stood, sparks crackling between her fingers. "I have plenty of power."

Power. "What if Amir suddenly had access to more power than he'd ever had before?" I asked. "He seems to be using quite a lot of time slips."

"Which are forbidden," Bennet reiterated.

"Not only are they forbidden, he's strong enough to move others," I said. "We have proof of that in the surveillance footage." I remembered a conversation I'd had with Dan, and asked, "When Amir was messing around with that portal in Iran, what was he doing?"

"He claimed that he didn't learn enough to truly do anything with it," Dad replied. "However, recent events make me want to revisit that case."

"Then we have two issues," Bennet said. "Hassan's usage of forbidden spell-craft, and the question of where he obtained this additional power. Despite his past opening of the portal, I don't believe it could be used as a power source."

"How do seers power up?" Dan asked.

I looked at my father, and he shrugged. "We don't, not really," I said. "We respond to the spirits around us."

Dan nodded. "Then he must be powering up like a witch."

We all looked at Tessa. "He could be obtaining power in several ways," she began. "The fastest ways to increase one's power are through sacrifice, either by blood or by soul."

"Is blood sacrifice what I think it is?" Dan asked.

Tessa nodded. "It is."

"But that's not what's happening," I said. "Witches are all about ancestors, and now Amir has the London clans in his pocket, and he went after Jada because she has Sarah Allwood's memories. He's holding a bunch of dead witches hostage." I looked at my father. "Nathaniel told me that Sarah was gone. What if Amir has her? What if he has other witches, too? If he's feeding on their energy, he could destroy them, permanently."

Dad nodded. "As seers, we must protect the dead as we do the living. Once we stop Amir, and preserve their ancestors' legacy, no witch will ever question your right to lead ever again."

Chapter 27

Toxic Bananas

Since Bennet had the necessary information, he set about contacting the witch clans to set up a meeting between them and me. I didn't know how the elders would react to me asking for their support. Hell, I didn't know if any of them would even show up at this meeting. I'd never even met most of them, and those who were aware of my existence knew me only as Helena Moore's granddaughter, or worse, the kid who'd gotten kidnapped by the Beauclaires.

I looked down at what I was wearing: a gauzy peasant top, denim shorts, and sandals. Add to my extremely casual attire the ponytail on top of my head, and I looked like I was on my way to a picnic in the park, not to a gathering that would hopefully name me as the new Mistress of Seers. While my clothes wouldn't change who I was or what I could do, Gran had taught me that appearances mattered, and how to work them to my advantage.

"I'm going home to change," I announced.

Tessa glanced at my outfit. "Good idea. Wear the navy blue."

I scrunched up my nose. "Really?"

"Do you want to look powerful or look good?" she countered.

"A little of both would be nice," I muttered. "I'll be back in an hour."

I left the office as Dan jogged to catch up to me. "I'll drive. And if we see Hassan on the way, I'll run him over."

"Good plan."

When we got in the car, Dan said, "Tell me about your father and Tessa. Exactly how on-again, off-again are they?"

"Dad and Tess are one of the great mysteries of the universe," I replied. "They love each other deeply, and probably always will. They're also mad at each other, but each one is more hurt than mad, and will also probably remain that way until the end of time."

"Why don't they just talk about it?"

"Oh, they talk all the time. They talk to themselves, each other, and to anyone else who will listen. Get three glasses of wine into Tessa and you'll learn details you never wanted to know."

"No, thank you. What did your grandmother think about the two of them being together?"

"Gran adored Tess. They'd been friends for years before my grandparents even met. Then Tessa went back to Europe, and when she returned, Dad was in his twenties."

"No one thought their age difference was odd?"

"That's the thing with witches and seers to a certain degree. Magic usage keeps your body in top condition, so the more you use magic, the longer you live, and the more youthful you appear. That means age differences, even huge honking age differences, are pretty common."

"Huge and honking," Dan repeated, and I giggled. "Is that what we have, a huge honking age difference?"

"I don't think so. Besides, my birthday's coming up."

Dan steered around a rotary. "How is it that your mother was unaware of her witchyness, for lack of a better term, yet she kept you after learning she was a witch while carrying you, only to freak out and disappear after all that happened when you were eight?"

I shrugged. "Like Dad said, she was born in an orphanage. She didn't know her own family history."

"Something's not right. She didn't know Alex was a seer? He doesn't seem like the kind of guy who hides what he is."

"He's not." I bit my lip. "What are you saying?"

"Not sure yet, but there's something more here. I don't think Alex or Tess are hiding anything, and Bennet's got so much information floating around in his brain I'm surprised he remembers how to tie his shoes, but you and me have an advantage they don't."

"What's that?"

"We're detectives. We see patterns where other people don't."

"And what is this pattern telling you?"

"That it hasn't yet revealed all its secrets."

We parked a block away from my apartment. The walk from the car to the stairs was one of the most tense experiences of my life; I kept expecting Amir to leap out from behind a bush or a lamppost like an extra in a low-quality horror movie. Cheap jump scares were definitely his style.

As soon as we were inside my place, Dan made a beeline toward the kitchen. "I am tossing your toxic bananas."

"Stop judging my fruit." I went to my closet and started digging for the navy blue dress Tess had suggested. It was a bit frumpy, but Tess did have a few hundred years of fashion expertise on me.

"Did you throw them out?" Dan yelled from the kitchen.

"What?"

"The bananas. They're... wait, they're yellow again?"

Shit. "Dan get down!"

Dan dove toward the bedroom doorway as I dropped to the floor. A shock wave of blue energy sliced through the apartment, destroying everything it came into contact with. I glanced at the scorch marks on the wall.

The line of destruction was about five feet high. I'm five foot three.

The spell had been cast to kill me.

"Are you okay?" I elbow walked to Dan, and ran my hands over his arms and back. "Any cuts, burns?"

"I'm in one piece. You?"

"I'm okay." My knee throbbed where I'd landed on it, but I assumed that would fade.

"What the hell just happened?"

"You know how Amir's been using time shifts? When you said the bananas were yellow again, it made me realize he'd been here, doing something. Laying a trap." I stared at the burnt scar that marked my walls and had cut my bedroom door in half. "This type of spell takes a long time to set, so he must have shifted time to make sure he was alone. In the process, he un-rotted the bananas."

"If we'd been standing, we'd be dead." Dan's face was bloodless, but his jaw was set. "Think he's close by?"

"Maybe. He's arrogant enough to assume the trap worked, and vain enough to come see the destruction for himself." I heard sirens in the distance, and hoped they weren't coming here. I didn't want any other innocents getting hurt.

"We need to move," Dan said, then he grabbed a piece of door and tossed it into the kitchen. When nothing incinerated it, he asked, "This spell a one-off?"

"Let's hope. Stay behind me."

I looped my bag across my body—it held almost everything in the apartment that was important to me—and crept out of the bedroom. We went toward the office door, instead of the one we'd come in. It was closer, and that way we could avoid the kitchen. I also wanted to grab my laptop, and my potted belladonna, just in case. Dan walked with his back to mine, gun raised.

Prudence, my judgmental ghost friend, appeared in front of me. "Don't go that way!" she shrieked.

"Why not?"

"There was a man here, and he unwound time," Prudence replied. "He spelled that door, too."

I squinted at the office door and saw the same telltale blue residue that had cracked my witchfinder smeared along the hinges. "Pru, do you know how he worked the spells?"

She shook her head. "All I know is it took him days. Destruction is woven around you like a spider's web."

"Dan." I put my hand on his shoulder. "We're trapped."

"I don't accept that."

"The door, everything is spelled!"

"What about the windows? The floor?" Dan grasped my hand. "Don't you dare give up."

"I'm not giving up. I just need to think."

"We'll think together. What do seers do?"

"I talk to the dead. I summon spirits. I hold the line between life and death. I keep the balance."

"What do witches do?" When I didn't answer, he added. "You're half witch. Use it."

Use it. "Witches manipulate energy. They're attuned to the earth. They—we—can alter things with our intentions." I remembered Jacob's lesson. "Magic is based on intent and emotion."

"I got emotions to spare. What's your intent?"

My gaze fell on the waiting room couch, the same couch where Nathaniel Beauclaire had tried to seduce me, but my tattoo had warned me away from him.

Nathaniel was stronger than Amir. He had the knowledge and power to counter any spell Amir had woven without breaking a sweat—but would he? Nathaniel's life would be easier without me ruining his plans... but he said he needed me to find Jada. Without the knowledge trapped inside Jada's head, he couldn't retrieve his wife from wherever Sarah had stashed her spirit.

I glanced at the office door. If I also summoned Amir, Nathaniel would be focused on him instead of whatever I was doing. With both of them distracted, Dan and I might have enough time to get out.

I touched the blue residue on the office door. "Amir Hassan! Amir, I summon you! Come to me now!"

Amir materialized next to me. He looked just the same as he always had, with his shiny dark hair and wide, sparkling grin. The things I used to do just to see that smile.

"Summoning spells," Amir said. "My, Ellie, you've come a long way."

I put my hand on my leg, right over the tattoo Nathaniel had touched. "Nathaniel Beauclaire, I summon you," I shouted. "Get your skinny ass here, now!"

Nathaniel appeared in front of us. "How—" He glanced at my destroyed apartment, and said, "Have we been redecorating?"

Instead of answering his question, I said, "Nathaniel, why don't you ask Amir about Jada."

Nathaniel's eyes flamed, and Amir backed up a step. Dan grabbed my hand, and we ran out of the kitchen door and down the back stairs.

"What are they gonna do to each other?" Dan asked.

The ground rumbled. "Nothing good!"

Dan opened his mouth, but it was too late. We'd only just gotten across the street when the northwest corner of the building blew clean off.

My home was gone.

Dan made a call, and said, "Lyons. I need the fire department, bomb squad, everything. There's been an explosion at the corner of Main and Pleasant with unknown casualties."

While Dan coordinated search and rescue, I stared at the empty corner where my apartment and business used to be. Black smoke billowed from the scorched brick work, mingling with steam from the burst pipes. It was a total loss. My computer, my clothes, even my stupid bananas were gone.

Nine Lives Investigations was my first real stab at adulthood, my first attempt at becoming something more than what everyone told me I was born to be. My first attempt at becoming me.

For my whole life, people had gone on about my supposed destiny. Dad, Gran, and everyone else had told me about the great power that awaited me, and that I needed to study hard and be disciplined in order to be a good leader. Well, I had studied, and I had been disciplined, and I still ended up kidnapped and stuffed in a basement when I was seventeen.

I left this life behind, but when Gran got sick, I came back. I was needed, and I had responsibilities. And what had that gotten me? Nothing. My life was a pile of ashes.

I clenched my fist so hard my nails cut into my palm.

Screw this. Screw all of this.

As of this moment, I was making the rules.

"You know what I hate?" I demanded.

Dan lowered his phone. "What's that?"

"Destiny. I hate it. I fucking hate it," I screamed at the sky, my fists clenched. My skin was streaked with ash and dust, and I could taste smoke in the back of my throat. "This is not fair!"

No one except Dan heard my tantrum, since the firetrucks and ambulances picked that moment to arrive. Dan glanced at them, and slid his phone into his back pocket.

"Don't you need to talk to them?" I asked.

"I'm not a fireman. I'll just be in the way." He stepped closer to me. He was covered in so much dust his black hair had gone salt and pepper. "I believe in making your own destiny. What do you want to do?"

I looked at the empty space that was once my future for the last time. "I am going to make Amir wish he had never messed with me. Let's head to Gran's."

CHAPTER 28

YOU SAVE ME, AND I SAVE YOU

"No, keep working on this meet up," I said. I'd called Dad from the car; it was better that he heard about my apartment's recent and total destruction directly from me instead of seeing it on the news. "I'm stopping by Gran's for clothes."

"You're certain you're okay?" Dad asked.

"We're okay. We got out in time." Gravel crunched under the tires as Dan pulled into Gran's driveway. "I'll call you when we're on our way."

"Be safe, Bug. Love you."

"Love you too, Dad."

When we got out of the car, Dan went to the back of the car and pulled a black duffle bag out from the tailgate. "What's in there?" I asked.

"Extra weapons, extra clothes, all sorts of stuff," he replied. "It's my 'if the world goes to hell in a handbasket' bag."

I nodded, then I spied a cluster of bleeding hearts growing next to the porch steps. It was as big and lush as all the others I'd seen across town, the bright pink blooms blazing in the sun.

These plants had driven me nuts, popping up out of nowhere and blooming out of season. Even though I now understood their meaning—and honestly, their presence had led to the best thing that had happened to me in a long time—I was on my last nerve, and wanted nothing more than to yank each and every one of them up by the roots and toss them into the compost heap. Instead of murdering the plants, I marched over to the closest bleeding heart and picked several flower stalks.

"Gathering a bouquet?" Dan asked. "That's my job."

"You can get the next one."

We went inside and were immediately accosted by the Feline Federation. I crouched down and said, "Guys, I need you to do something for me, and I need you to keep it a secret. Can you do that?" They lined themselves up in front of me, their furry little faces tilted upward with their tails wrapped around their feet, three proper little snoops. "Find Dad's kit."

The cats scampered off. "Come on. Let's get changed," I said, and Dan followed me upstairs and into my old room.

"This is where you grew up?" Dan asked, craning his neck to take in everything. We went up the main staircase, which was wide enough for four adults to walk up side by side, and was covered in a deep green carpet. When we got to the second floor, and all the associated polished woodwork and vintage crystal wall sconces, we took a left and entered the eastern wing of the house, which was my area. The front room was filled with upholstered furniture and heavy draperies. There was even a mahogany writing desk tucked into the corner.

"Not exactly a teenage paradise," Dan observed.

"This is just the sitting room. The bed's through here."

I led Dan into my old bedroom—my only bedroom, now that Amir had destroyed my apartment—and if the front room was a scene from Little Women, the bedroom was decorated in full Jane Austen splendor. The centerpiece of the room was a large fourposter bed, complete with a frilly white canopy. To the left was a dark wood vanity and bench, and to the right were two freestanding wardrobes in a matching finish. All in all, it looked like the queen slept here.

"I stand corrected. You grew up in a museum."

"In more ways than one." I opened one of the wardrobes and took stock of the clothes I had to work with. There were jeans, tee shirts, and some truly scandalous dresses. At least nothing was moth eaten. "I am going to go to the most important meeting of my life dressed like someone's disaffected niece."

Dan draped his arm around my shoulders. "So what? You look great in jeans." I laughed and let him pull me into his arms. "You sure you're okay?"

"I am very much not okay," I said into his chest. "I am mad, and filthy, and homeless, and I will deal with all of that later. Right now, we have work to do."

I pulled away before the dust made me sneeze into his shirt. "Want to wash up? Bathroom's this way."

I entered the bathroom, which was as opulent and old-fashioned as the rest of the house. The walls were completely covered in cream tile, with a dark green border along the floor, and matching ornate floral Art Deco tiles lined up against the ceiling. The far wall was taken up with a huge stained glass window representing some of Gran's favorite plants. Two sinks with matching mirrors took up one side of the room, while the wall opposite the window was where the clawfoot tub lived. I'd spent half of my youth hiding in that tub, wishing it was a ship that could take me to a far-off world.

Today I wasn't as interested in the tub as the shower, and grateful that Gran had made the enhancement. Actually, I'd whined about the lack of a shower until she hired a plumber, but that's another story.

I turned on the shower so the water could heat up, then I took stock of the toiletries. There were a few of my old items that had been sitting around for over a year, along with some new bottles Dad must have brought with him. Since he tended to scoop up whatever was free or cheap, regardless of the ingredients, I decided to leave those alone.

"Dan," I called. "Don't you want to shower?"

"I thought I'd give you some space."

"Space is the last thing I need."

I stripped and got under the spray, and watched the dust and grime rinse off me and pool in the bottom of the tub. Dan pulled back the curtain, and I jerked my chin toward the gray puddle. "As you can see, I was filthy."

"What you are is gorgeous." Dan got in the tub and found the body wash. "Turn around. I'll do your back."

We went on that way, taking turns washing each other in a very non-sexy yet intimate way. I'd never felt closer to anyone in my life, and this closeness reinforced an idea I'd first had when I picked the bleeding hearts next to the porch. I only hoped Dan would agree to go along with my plan.

Once we were as clean as we were going to get, we toweled off and returned to the bedroom. "What's the next move?" Dan asked.

"We wait for Dad or Tess to call." I sat on the bed. "They're working on setting up the meeting with the elders. We're on our own until then." He sat next to me, and I realized something. "Since I've lived here, no one has ever been on this bed except me. I've never had a sleepover, or had a boyfriend stop by."

"Really?" He leaned on his elbow. "Early training for your nun career?"

"Believe me, I wanted boyfriends and sleepovers, but I didn't get any of that. It would have been awkward, explaining why there was a room full of poisons next to the kitchen, and a parlor full of witches downstairs. And now, you're here."

"Wait, so I'm your first?"

"Guess so." I leaned over to kiss him, but Pumpkin jumped onto the bed between us.

"Hey, fluff. Did you find it?" She put her calico paw on my hand. "Good girl. Give us a minute." I got up, and said, "I'm going to get dressed. There's something I need to do, and I'd rather not be naked." I paused, my hand on the wardrobe's door. "I'm hoping you'll help me."

"You know I'll do anything for you."

Thus heartened, I picked out some clothes. I ended up wearing jeans, boots, a black tee shirt, and yet another plaid button down shirt. Apparently, teenaged Eli had really wanted to be a lumberjack. Dan's comment on me looking good in jeans may or may not have influenced my wardrobe choices. He was also wearing jeans, boots, and a black short sleeved shirt, which he accessorized with a shoulder holster.

"You look like a cop," I said.

"I am a cop. You look like the next indie rock sensation."

I smiled. The next time we showered together I'd sing and thus disabuse him of that notion. "Come on. Pumpkin's got something to show us."

I grabbed the bleeding heart stalks from where I'd left them on the vanity, then Dan and I followed Pumpkin out of the room and down the hall. She passed by my father's room, and went straight to the library at the back of the house.

"I have a question," Dan announced, when we were about halfway down the hall.

"Ask away."

"If you only come by to water the plants, and Alex is always traveling, who cleans this place?"

I glanced around the hall. The wood paneling shone as if it had been freshly polished, and all of the wall sconces sparkled like diamonds. "Family lore says that a witch had a crush on my great-great-grandmother, and he cast a maintenance spell on the house as a grand gesture of his affection. Since that day, we haven't had a speck of dust or muddy footprint to speak of."

Dan grunted. "Think Tess can cast one of those spells on my place?"

"She might, if you ask nicely."

We reached the library's door. After Pumpkin slipped inside, I pushed it open and took a moment to appreciate the room. The solarium would always be my favorite room in the house, but the library was a close second. It was like something out of a medieval monastery with floor to ceiling bookcases, and several desks stocked with paper and pencils. There was even a spiral staircase in the far corner, which led to the house's cupola.

Dan pointed toward the spiral stairs. "Where does that go?"

"It leads to a cupola. We don't go up there."

We entered the library, and found Dad's marksman kit laid atop a table. Smokey and Muffuletta sat on either side, guarding the leather satchel like sphinxes.

"Good job, guys. I knew I could count on you." As I opened up the satchel, the cats filed out the door.

"Are you sure they aren't alive?" Dan asked.

"I'm not sure of anything these days." I started withdrawing items from Dad's kit and setting them out on the table. There was a mortar and pestle, several tiny vessels of ink, and a set of wickedly sharp needles.

"What's all this?" Dan asked, eyeing the needles.

"Dad's the seer's marksman. This is his kit."

"Are you planning on giving yourself a tattoo?"

I faced Dan. "I was hoping I could give you one."

Dan glanced at my face, and back at the needles. "I'm gonna need a little more of an explanation than that."

"Okay." I paced the length of the table and back, struggling to find the words to what I knew to be true in my bones. "At my place, you saw me summon Nathaniel and Amir."

"I did."

"I shouldn't be able to do that. I can summon the dead, and those two are very much alive. That should not have worked, yet it did. Twice."

"Could the residual magic from that daisy cutter spell Amir left us have, I don't know, amplified you?"

"That's a possibility," I conceded. "But I've done other things that should have been impossible, too. Jacob's spirit, for one, and the time I harnessed the Allwood ancestors and fed you their energy."

"Alex said your mother made flowers spring up wherever she walked, and you created a bleeding heart epidemic," Dan added.

I felt my face warm. "We caused the bleeding hearts, but yeah. Same concept."

Dan nodded. "How does any of that tie into me getting a tattoo?"

"I think the witch side of me enhances the seer, and vice versa. Jacob said that magic is all about intent and emotion. Every time I want something and put feeling behind it, it happens." I touched Dan's forearm. "When we were trapped in the Allwoods' basement, you were so weak I didn't know if you'd make it. I couldn't carry you, and you weren't waking up, and I was freaking out... And then I was drawing on dozens of dead ancestors and they helped me make you whole again. I wanted you to wake up, and be strong, and you were."

Dan cupped my cheek with his hand. "It was that bad?"

I took a breath and covered his hand with my own. "Yeah. I never told you how far gone you were, but I really didn't think you were going to survive all of that." I squeezed my eyes shut, trying to stop the memory of Dan beaten nearly to death from surfacing. "Ever since then, I've been different."

"Different how?"

"My panic attacks are almost completely gone. I used to have them a few times a week, sometimes twice or three times a day. After that time in the basement, I've had exactly one panic attack, and it was when you were possessed."

Dan rested his forehead against mine. "I'm different too. I'm calmer at work, the chief hasn't written me up in months, and... And I look forward to waking up in the morning. I look forward to each day." He kissed my knuckles. "I have hope again."

"I think it's what Jacob called us, the circle unbroken. Tess said it's a witch term for soulmates. We replenish each other."

He pressed another kiss to my knuckles. "You save me, and I save you."

"That's the thing. I can't keep saving you. Eventually someone like Amir will realize what's happening, decide you're my weakness and exploit it. That means you need an edge."

"What kind of an edge?"

"I want to give you a seer's mark, so you can see and communicate with ghosts, too."

Dan moved his fingers to my wrist, and rubbed his thumb across my mark. "Will that work?"

"I think so. I think if my intent is to give you a mark that will allow you to see spirits, and I put all the emotions I feel for you into it, I think it will work."

"All these emotions, huh?" He stroked his thumb over the thin inner skin of my wrist. "It took over a year for you to admit you like me."

"What can I say. You're the smart one." I closed my eyes. "You've already been hurt so much because of me, by people you who never should have gone near you. I don't know if I could take it if you got hurt again. I need you to be safe, and while part of me wants to lock you in a room until this is all over, I know that wouldn't be fair to you. I need to give you the means to keep yourself safe."

Dan was silent as my heart hammered in my chest. That was the closest I'd ever come to baring my heart to anyone. Everything I'd said was true. He meant so much to me, and him being near me meant he would always be in danger. If anything more happened to him, I didn't know what I would do.

"Let me get this straight. If I let you tattoo me, I'll have superpowers like you?"

I peeked up at him, saw him smiling. "These are not superpowers."

"Says the woman with the powers. I'll do it on one condition. You tattoo me, and I get to kiss you whenever I want."

I blinked. "Really? You'll do it?"

"Yes, but not because of whatever edge I might get. I'll do it because I can use this power to keep you safe, too." He looked at the needles and frowned. "Will this hurt?"

I shrugged. "Probably. All of mine did."

He sighed, or maybe it was more of a groan. "All right. Let's get this show on the road."

I stood on my toes and kissed him. "You're the best."

We sat at the table, and I spread out Dad's tools. I'd watched him make inks and give tattoos at least a hundred times. I knew exactly what to do, yet I only sat there, staring.

"How do we start?" Dan asked, snapping me out of my trance.

Trance.

"I need to meditate, and let your mark come to me." I took his left hand in both of mine and held it palm up on the table. "Meditate with me?"

"Sure," he replied; based on his tone of voice, I was certain Dan had never meditated a single moment in his life. Good thing he was a fast learner. "What do I do?"

"Nothing. Just clear your mind and see what happens."

I closed my eyes and let everything go; every worry, every insecurity, every nagging thought and little voice that told me I wasn't good enough. That I would never fill Gran's shoes, that I was a poor excuse for a seer. That my mother had left because I wasn't good enough for her.

What if she hadn't been good enough for me?

I banished that thought, but at the last moment, I called it back. My mother had abandoned me, that much was true. But what if she hadn't run to hurt me? What if she'd left in order to save me?

What if she'd always known she was a witch, and that was the key to all of this?

"Key, key, key," I muttered.

"What's that, babe?"

"Nothing. Just thinking out loud," I replied, then I delved back into my thoughts. If my witch blood is the key, that means there's a lock. What does it open?

I felt Dan's hand, lightly running my fingers over his skin. His palms were calloused and rough, but underneath it all, his skin was soft. I dragged my fingertip over the center of his palm and stifled a giggle when he flinched. He was strong, reliable, and ticklish. He complemented me in every way, just as I complemented him.

We fit together perfectly.

He was the lock. I am the key.

What do I unlock?

"Potential."

I released Dan's hand, unfolded a square of blue silk from Dad's kit and put the bleeding heart stalks on top of it, then I set the mortar and pestle behind the fabric. Once everything was arranged, I began picking apart the flowers, organizing the petals and leaves by color.

"How can I help?"

"I need to do this part," I mumbled. I scooped up the pink petals and dumped them in the mortar, then I started crushing them.

"Does this mean my tattoo will be pink?"

I glanced up, saw his brow pinched with concern. "The petals are just an ingredient. It'll be blue, like mine."

"Oh. I like blue."

Once I judged that the petals were thoroughly pulverized, I added a few drops of the lapis lazuli ink. Dad had made that ink special when he first became the marksman, and had only ever used it on himself and me. He claimed the ink was more powerful than the rest, and power was exactly what I needed.

"I'm going to paint the design on your skin first, then we'll move on to needles." I dipped a brush into the ink mixture.

"Do I get a say in the design?"

"It will be a lock."

"Any reason?"

"Because I am the key to unlocking your magical potential." I brushed on the outline of a padlock. "One of the very first things Gran taught me was that everyone has unlimited potential. When we put people in categories, like seer or witch or mortal, we're just assigning labels. It's a human thing to categorize what's around us. Our brains are wired that way."

"But she unwired you?"

"In a way, yes. She was adamant that the labels are meaningless, and that anyone can become adept with any form of magic they choose." A final sweep of my brush, and I completed the tiny padlock on Dan's wrist. "With this mark, I aim to unlock your potential."

"For magic?"

"For whatever you want."

I met his gaze and realized something. Dan trusted me, not only with his heart and body, but with all of the parts of himself he had yet to understand. He trusted me with his soul, and it was the best gift he ever could have given me.

And I would repay that gift with pain. At least it would be over soon.

"This next bit won't be fun," I said as I picked up a needle. "Have you ever been stung by a bee?"

Chapter 29

Foresight And Time Slips

"That did not feel like a bee sting," Dan said. Again.

"Sorry. It was my first tattoo," I said, also again. "Don't worry, I'm sure my technique will improve after I've done a few more."

"You're not practicing on me," he muttered. "Once was enough."

I glanced at him, but stayed quiet. I remembered how sore I'd been after some of Dad's marathon tattoo sessions, and how he'd let me whine about it. The least I could do was offer the same courtesy to Dan.

"When does this new spirit vision kick in?" Dan asked.

"Not sure," I said. "Do you sense anything new? Unusual?"

"Aside from the throbbing pain in my wrist," he began, then he cocked his head to the side. "There's something downstairs."

"Really?" I asked. I knew exactly what he was sensing, but that wasn't the point. "Follow it."

"Follow what?"

"It."

Dan followed the sensation down to the first floor, through the front parlor and into Gran's solarium. "It's in here, somewhere."

"What's in here?"

"The thing," he said, exasperation making him raise his voice. "The it. It's calling me... pulling me toward something. Toward it."

He turned around in a complete circle, staring at the plants, the ceiling, and even the bookcases. When he stopped moving, his gaze landed on Pumpkin.

"Hey, kitty," he said, then he paused. "It's her."

"What's her?"

"Pumpkin. She's the it." He gasped, and said, "She's the spirit. She doesn't look real anymore. I mean, she's real, but not alive. I see the difference between her, and you and me." Dan picked Pumpkin up and rubbed behind her ears. "I can tell that she's a spirit."

"Look at you," I began, then my phone buzzed. I withdrew it and saw it was Dad. I accepted the call, and said, "I used your kit." Like ripping off a Band-Aid, it was best to get confessions over with quickly.

"I know."

"You do?"

"I knew the moment you touched it."

"Why didn't you run over here screaming for me to stop?"

"Because I've always trusted you to do the right thing. Also, Tessa refused to drive me."

"Thanks, Dad. You really are the best."

"As are you. Bennet has set up the meeting."

Dad gave me the details of my meeting with the witch elders. When I ended the call, I turned around and saw Dan sitting on the chaise with all three of the cats draped across him.

"Play time's over," I said to him as much as the cats. "Meeting's on."

According to Dad, Bennet had called in all of his favors to arrange a meeting between the elders of the six witch clans and myself. It would be taking place at Potter's Field on the outskirts of town, which was conveniently equidistant from five of the six clan homes. The Beauclaires technically didn't have a home any longer, since my father had destroyed the last one. I suppose Nathaniel's home could be considered the clan's home base, though I would rather be homeless than claim him as my leader. Then again, I was currently homeless, and Nathaniel was partly to blame.

Ugh. I hoped all of this would be over soon.

Dan and I said goodbye to the cats, locked up Gran's house, and drove toward the field.

"Is your father meeting us there?" Dan asked.

"I think so." We turned onto the road that led to the field, and I saw people standing in the center of the grassy area. "It looks like we aren't the first to arrive. They're early."

"Doesn't matter. Show won't start until you get there." Dan glanced at me and grinned. Then the road buckled, and the car flipped onto its roof.

The next thing I knew, I was hanging upside down in my seat, my head dazed and ears ringing as if a bomb had gone off. My thoughts were muddled, and I had no idea what had happened. I glanced out what was left of the front window, saw an empty field.

Where were the people?

I smelled smoke. Fire? I looked to my left, and saw Dan hanging upside down and unresponsive, with a smear of blood across his forehead.

"Dan," I said, but I couldn't hear myself over the ringing in my ears. "Dan, wake up!"

The sight of Dan hurt cut through the haze in my mind. This event was exactly what my foresight had warned me about.

I withdrew a knife from my boot and cut through my seatbelt, then I shimmied out of my seat. We'd landed on the SUV's roof, so I crawled into the back and kicked out the rear window. Escape route secured, I cut Dan loose from his seatbelt and dragged him out through the back window.

"You weigh a ton," I said. I couldn't hear myself, and Dan was unconscious, but talking to him made me feel like I was accomplishing something. "You have got to go on a diet. Or maybe I need to work out. Once all of this is over, we can start lifting weights together."

I got Dan about ten feet away from the car before I collapsed onto the pavement. Was that far enough away from the vehicle? I had no idea. What I did know what that smoke was everywhere, but neither the car nor the field was on fire. What's more, there was no other vehicle present, or large animal crossing the road, or badly positioned tree or rock. This was a single vehicle accident.

"Why did we crash?" I looked at the SUV; all four of the tires were in the air, but they didn't look damaged. I took a breath and noted the absolute lack of a burnt odor. We weren't surrounded by smoke, but an unusually thick fog. "How did we flip?"

I squinted into the pea soup-like fog. That accomplished exactly nothing, so I stood and gathered my intent. I clapped my hands together like I'd seen Tessa do so many times, and said, "Clarity."

The fog dissipated, along with the haze in my mind and the ringing in my ears. Evil magic fog, then. What fun. I pulled out my phone and called my father.

"Hey, Bug."

"Dad, where are you?"

"I'm right where you left me ten minutes ago."

Cold dread formed a ball in my stomach. "We left the school hours ago. Dan and I are here with—"

I turned toward the empty field. "Dad, Amir's at Potter's Field. He used a time shift and did something to us. The clan elders were here!"

I heard Dad talking to Tess and Bennet, then he said to me, "Stay there. We're coming to you."

My foresight tingled the back of my neck. "No! Stay away," I yelled, but Dad had already hung up. I tried calling him back, but couldn't get a signal.

"Stupid phone," I muttered.

From behind me, a man said, "Pity that you're all alone out here."

I'd know that voice anywhere. I used to crave the sound of it, go through with morally questionable and downright awful schemes just to hear it praise me.

But that was the old me, the Ellie that craved Amir's attention and approval. Now I am Eliza Moore, Mistress of Seers, and I am done with Amir's shit.

"Amir Hassan, you are not welcome here." I faced him, fists clenched at my sides. "The Northeastern Clans did not invite you, nor are you welcome to remain. Be gone, and do not return."

"Last I checked, this was a free country," he said. "I can be wherever I like."

"You are trespassing, by our laws and the laws of mortals," I added, since I was pretty sure he didn't have a passport or any other legal identification. "Leave now, or there will be consequences."

"Consequences," Amir balked. "What consequences? You can't even drive yourself down a road properly. What could you do to me?"

He's stalling. "Vision," I intoned, and I could see in a full three hundred sixty degree circle. It was disorienting, and Amir sneered when I stumbled, but I ignored him. Unlike when I'd last associated with Amir, I wasn't trying to impress him.

Then I saw the Ghost Guys creeping up behind me.

I didn't want to face them and turn my back on Amir, so I focused on Dan and said, "Awake and alert!"

"What... what happened?" Dan sat up, rubbing his temple.

"Ghost Guys at my five o'clock," I said. I heard Dan draw his gun and tell them to halt, then I refocused on Amir.

Only Amir wasn't in front of me.

"Is this Dan?" Amir said. He'd somehow gone from right in front of me to standing between Dan and the Ghost Guys in the blink of an eye. "I assumed so when he was at your apartment. My, Ellie, now that I'm seeing him up close, I really, really don't understand the attraction."

"Don't you dare," I said, raising my knife.

"Don't I dare what? Say hello? I feel like we're past that. I've already been inside him." Amir sneered. "Right before I was inside you."

"He's lying," I said. "He wants to rattle us."

"Me? Tell an untruth?" Amir asked in mock offense. "Ellie, you wound me."

"Where's Jada?" Dan demanded, his gun trained on Amir.

"Safe, as are her secrets," Amir replied. "You really should be worried, Ellie. The information in that girl's mind can ruin every clan on this continent, maybe the world."

Why does he care about ruining clans? I didn't believe that was Amir's sole motive. He had many flaws, one of which was his total disdain for authority. His biggest flaw was his ambition. "Are you supposed to be using time shifts?"

Amir blinked. "What?"

"You keep using time shifts. I don't think those are allowed." I concentrated on Jacob Allwood; since he was a spirit, it was easy to summon him. When Jacob appeared beside me, Amir stepped back in shock.

"Eliza, what's happening here?" Jacob asked.

"Jacob, you told me someone threatened you," I said. "Was that threat made by one Amir Hassan?"

"Why, yes." Jacob followed my gaze. "It was that fellow, right there. He threatened me."

"Amir is also using time shifts," I said. "Like, a lot of time shifts."

"That... that is not good," Jacob said.

"Aren't they forbidden?"

"Forbidden in that only a fool uses them," Jacob replied. "Altering the fabric of time has serious consequences. Time work is hardly taught any longer for that precise reason."

Then why is he using them? Amir had always dabbled in magic, and I wouldn't put it past him to deliberately seek out the most dangerous spells he could find. But everything he did was for a reason. He wouldn't bother learning something unless it fit into his plan.

Which meant that Jada hadn't been his sole target.

"He's going to shift Jada," I said, the pieces falling into place. "He doesn't want Jada's memories. He wants Sarah Allwood."

"We cannot allow that," Jacob said, then he paused. "What has happened to Dan?"

"I gave him a mark, so he's able to see spirits," I replied. "I unlocked his potential."

Jacob turned to me, his eyes wide. "How are you able to do these things?"

"She's half witch," Amir yelled. "I have the lineages! Eliza Moore is half witch, and the oldest law still practiced states that no seer with witch blood may rise to a position of authority!"

"He's right," Jacob murmured. "So, how do we get around this law?"

"You'll still support me?"

"Of course I will." Jacob faced Amir and raised his hands in a warding spell. "As a spirit, I shouldn't be leading my clan, either. We can be scofflaws together."

"Eli, incoming," Dan yelled. I had no idea what he meant until the air wavered, and the outlines of four other people shimmered into view.

"You didn't unlock Dan's potential to see spirits," Jacob said. "He senses all magic. In this case, Amir's working another time slip."

I decided to worry about Dan's unexpected upgrades later. I reached into the ether and grabbed the individuals from Amir, and let them materialize alongside myself and Jacob. They were the elders of the Howe, Wardwell, Burroughs, and Martin clans.

"You're safe from him," I said to the elders. "I won't let Amir harm you."

"He already has," a woman said. Jacob leaned close to my ear and murmured that her name was Melinda Howe. "He's fed our past selves' poison. If we support you as leader of the seers, he won't give us the antidote."

"We can make the antidote now," I said, but she shook her head.

"I fear it will be too late," Melinda said.

That's what he's been doing with the time slips. "Jacob, it might be just you and me," I said.

"And me." Nathaniel Beauclaire appeared beside us. "Hassan hasn't given me the poison."

"I thought you would've killed him at my place."

"I tried." Nathaniel speared me with his gaze. "Don't worry. I've never failed at anything twice."

I nodded, then I turned to the other four elders. "Clan Allwood and Clan Beauclaire are with me," I announced. "My father and I understand poisons and antidotes better than anyone else alive today. If you four agree to follow me as Mistress of Seers, I can save you from whatever Amir's done!"

The elders looked among themselves, then Melinda Howe said, "None of us will follow you, dear."

"I can stop Amir," I began, but she shook her head.

"It has nothing to do with Amir," she said. "It's because of your curse."

Chapter 30

Cursed

"My...what?"

"Well, yes." Melinda leaned closer to me. "Didn't you know about the curse, dear?"

Jacob lowered his glasses and stared into my eyes. "There is a thread of black magic inside you."

I glared at Nathaniel. "Why did you curse me?"

"Why do I get blamed for all your problems?" Nathaniel countered. "All I want is my wife restored to me. Whatever Hassan is doing is his own scheme."

"Your curse makes us unable to trust you," Melinda continued. "What if it takes over your mind, and you capture our ancestors? What if you drain their spirits and use your newfound power against us?"

"I would never do that," I said. "I can have the curse removed!"

Melinda shook her head. "Being that until a moment ago you were wholly ignorant of a curse we can all detect as plain as day, that begs the question of what else you're ignorant of. Leave us be, Eliza. We must support Amir."

"He'll kill you," I said. "He's probably lying about the antidote."

"That he may be," she conceded.

Panicked, I turned to Jacob. "What do I do?"

Jacob's gaze swept from the elders to Amir. "I believe we must withdraw, at least for the time being. Until we understand who cursed you, and how to remove it, those four will not follow you."

"I will not withdraw," I said, then I felt heat gathering in my palm. My anger had coalesced into a fireball, and I knew just where to throw it.

Nathaniel put himself between me and Amir. "Miss Moore, don't."

"You don't even know what I'm going to do."

"Don't be too certain of that." Nathaniel leaned closer and said, "If you murder Hassan in front of the elders, they'll never follow you. You may even be banished."

"They can't banish me!"

"They can," Jacob said. "Lower the flames, Eli. For me, please."

Jacob's plea reached the rational part of me, and the flames extinguished. "I won't let him win," I said. "What if I give the elders an antidote to whatever poisoned them?"

"If you do so, they will be grateful, but still wary," Nathaniel said. "Jacob is correct. The curse must be stripped from you. Only then will you have a chance at gaining their trust."

"But without them, who leads the seers?" I asked.

"I certainly won't follow Hassan," Nathaniel said.

"Nor will I," Jacob said. "We also won't decide anything standing in the street. Best to withdraw and regroup."

I didn't like it. In fact, I hated it, but Jacob and Nathaniel were right. Amir and I were at an impasse. I walked away from the elders and put my hand on Dan's shoulder. "It's over. Let's go."

"It is not over," Dan said. "That bastard tried to kill us!"

"Most of the elders won't follow me," I said. "Besides, if they betray Amir, he'll let them die."

Dan lowered his gun, and said softly, "Then maybe we save them from Amir, and they'll reevaluate their loyalties."

"How do we save them?"

"Don't know, but we can figure it out."

"Okay." It was a good plan, and while it galled me to let Amir have even this temporary victory, but it needed to be done. We needed to take a step back and reevaluate the situation. I was about to say as much to Amir, when Dan tensed.

"What's wrong?" I demanded.

"Magic incoming." His brow pinched. "A lot of it."

"More magic than is already here?" Between the six clan elders, myself, and Amir, there was more magic in Potter's Field than anywhere else for a hundred miles. Then a gray sports car sped into view, and skidded to a halt next to Dan's overturned SUV.

"Is Tessa or my dad the source of the magic?" I asked.

"It's both of them."

Tessa got out and stalked toward Amir, while Dad moved toward the clan elders. Dad tossed a web of protection spells over the elders—even Jacob and Nathaniel—while Tessa lobbed a ball of energy at Amir. The air crackled and smelled of ozone, then the ball shattered above Amir's head, and a shimmering white powder coated him.

"What was that?" I asked.

"A temporal binding," Tessa replied. "I've bound Amir to this time stream so he can only move forward. He won't be able to use time slips again."

Amir looked at the glistening powder on his hands, then he burst into laughter. "Thank you, Tess," he said. "Thank you very much for your assistance. Nathaniel, if you need me, I'll be with your girl."

Amir disappeared. For a moment I wondered how he'd done that, then I glanced at the clan elders, and the meaning behind his latest taunts hit me.

"Tess, Amir gave the elders poison, then he shifted them," I explained. "If he can't shift to their past selves with the antidote, they'll die."

Tessa gasped and covered her mouth. "I-I didn't know!"

"We'll figure this out." I looked toward the clan elders, four of whom Tessa had just inadvertently doomed. "Somehow."

CHAPTER 31

WE CAN HANDLE IT

BENNET POURED ANOTHER CUP of tea and said, "I'd say things have gone from bad to worse."

I accepted the cup. "You are not wrong."

A few days had passed since the debacle at Potter's Field. We were sitting in Bennet's office at the college, hiding out from the legions of pissed off witches. Not only was Amir now the unofficial leader of every seer in the world, soon enough the clan elders would perish and he would harness their spirits, and therefore, their entire clans. And that last part was all Tessa's fault.

She'd had the best of intentions when she crafted the temporal binding she used on Amir, and she'd made it as strong as she knew how. Being that Tessa was a highly skilled witch with centuries of experience, that meant the spell was as strong as steel. Unfortunately, her good intentions had played right into Amir's hands, since now he was unable to time shift to give the elders an antidote to whatever they'd been poisoned with. I questioned if he'd ever meant to save any of the elders, or if their deaths had always been part of his plan. Either way, ever since that day at the field, Tessa had been holed up with Dad while they tried to figure out how to undo her spell and keep the elders alive.

The biggest unknown was that we had no idea when Amir had poisoned the elders. Was it last week, last year, or sometime in the future? Poisons worked at different rates, and with different levels of toxicity. The elders might die today, tomorrow, or next week. Or maybe it had all been a lie, and Amir hadn't poisoned anyone. We just didn't know.

And then there was my curse.

"Did you know about the curse?" I asked.

"Yes, but not until after Helena had taken custody of you," he replied. "She didn't realize you were cursed until sometime after you went to live with to her, and she spent many years trying to undo it."

"Was I born with it?"

"No, you were not."

"Did Gran think my mother cursed me?"

"Yes, that was Helena's opinion."

I sighed. "My mother was really going for parent of the year."

"As much as Christina acted badly, also consider that she had virtually no magical training," Bennet said. "Whatever curse was delivered may have been done so accidentally, and she may not have considered it a curse at all. She may have been attempting to help you."

I knew Bennet was only trying to help, so I refrained from mentioning how an accidental cursing sounded like the plot to a lame sitcom about politically correct witches. Before he could further defend my absentee mother, the alarm on my phone beeped.

"I've got to pick up Dan." I stood and grabbed my keys. "Thanks for the tea."

"Of course. Please give my regards to Dan."

"Will do."

I hopped in my car and drove the short distance to the police station. Dan's SUV had been damaged beyond repair back at Potter's Field, which meant that I was on transport duty. I think he liked being chauffeured around a lot more than he let on.

When I got to the station, I nodded hello to the desk sergeant and went straight to Dan's desk. He wasn't there, so I sat in his chair and waited for him. It wasn't long before he appeared, carrying his usual armload of files. His face lit up when he saw me, and I tried not to blush.

"Hey, babe," he said. "That time already?"

"Sure is. Ready?"

"Let's go." He set down the files and grabbed his jacket, and I followed him back out to the parking lot.

"I've got Jill running a trace on your mother," he said, as he sat in the passenger seat. "There can't be that many Christina Louise Linds in this area. We'll find her."

"And then what?"

"And then we'll ask her some questions and follow the facts wherever they take us."

I pulled out of the parking lot and turned toward Dan's place. I'd been hanging out at his house for the past few nights, and it had been fun staying with him. Last night we'd even cooked dinner together. It had been a mess, and mostly burnt, and proved that neither one of us was meant to be a chef.

That was fine with me. I much preferred solving mysteries to chopping vegetables.

"What if we don't like her answers?" I asked, since I was fairly certain my mother—if we found her—wouldn't tell us anything good.

"Even if the answers she gives us aren't good ones, they can still point us in the right direction." He set his hand on top of mine. "Don't worry about her. We can handle anything she throws at us."

I turned my hand over and laced my fingers with Dan's. A circle unbroken, that's exactly what we were. "Yeah. We can."

I hope you enjoyed reading about Eli and Dan's latest adventures! If so, please consider leaving a review at the retailer where you purchased this book. Thank you!

The story continues in Thornapple, available here: https://books2read.co m/poisongarden-thornapple. Keep scrolling for a sneak peek!

THORNAPPLE

Dan shook his head. "I don't know about this."

"Do you have a better idea?" I countered.

He frowned. "No."

"Neither do I."

Our current questionable idea was to have me sit under the light of the full moon while Tessa examined me and tried to glean some information about my curse. Since this curse hadn't been present when I was born, and Gran hadn't detected it on me until I was eight, it could have come from anyone and anywhere—but I was dead certain this was my mother's handiwork. Let's just say she's never been in the running for parent of the year.

In order to accomplish this feat of curse detection, Tessa, Dan, and I were in Dan's backyard setting up a magic circle on his well-tended lawn. Luckily, he wasn't one of those fools who opted for the lawn care company that doused its clients' yards in chemicals to keep the grass green for longer than it was meant to be. Since this sort of ritual was best conducted with the subject—in this case, me—in direct contact with the earth, his freshly trimmed lawn was an ideal location.

Gran's yard would have also been a good place, mostly because the earth there knew me, and the familiar setting would offer an extra bit of protection. But my father was there, searching every spell book and grimoire he could find, and this spell required me to be completely naked. While I didn't mind nudity, being a grown woman naked in front of my dad was something to be avoided at all costs. Besides, Dan had a nice tall stockade fence, which would keep out the neighbors' prying eyes.

"It's ready," Tessa said. She'd drawn a circle of salt on the lawn, and set five white pillar candles at the cardinal points. "I even brought you a pillow," she added, indicating the purple cushion in the middle of the circle.

"You're so good to me." I kicked off my sandals, then I pulled my shirt off and handed it to Dan.

"Do we all need to be naked for this?" he asked.

"Only if you'd like to be," Tessa purred.

"Tess," I admonished, "stop trying to embarrass him." I slipped off my shorts and handed them to my increasingly flustered partner. I had to admit, Dan was pretty cute when he blushed. He frowned at my bare body, then he leaned over and kissed my temple.

"Anything goes sideways, yell," he said. "I'll have you out of that circle in a hot second."

I gripped his hand, as much to reassure myself as him. "Tessa won't let anything happen to me."

With that, I stepped inside the circle and sat cross-legged in the center, my butt on the cold grass while the cushion supported my back. Once I was seated, Tess entered the circle and poured out the last measure of salt, thus closing the spell around us. She snapped her fingers, and the five candles lit as one.

"Whoa," Dan said.

Tessa glanced at Dan and grinned, then she focused on me. "You know how this goes," she began. "Clear your mind, but make note of any stray thoughts, especially persistent ones."

"Got it." I shook out my arms. "Are you starting with my head?"

"Your fingers, actually," Tessa replied, then she grasped my left hand and began probing the skin between my fingers.

"Are finger curses common?" Dan asked.

"It depends on the purpose of the curse." Having finished with my left hand, Tessa scrutinized my wrist, then my forearm. "If you want to impede someone's ability to write, or perhaps play an instrument, the fingers would be an ideal location."

Dan grunted. I flashed him a smile and let my eyes close. The spell intensified, making my limbs feel like warm molasses. "This feels nice," I mumbled.

"Don't get too comfortable," Tessa warned. "I need you to stay awake."

I nodded, but I felt my consciousness drifting farther away. Tessa's fingers were hypnotic as they glided across my skin, the soft thrum of her magic soothing my soul. But even as I was soothed, something deep within me woke up.

Something that didn't want to be found.

I tried to tell Tessa, but my throat was thick, my tongue heavy. I didn't know if she'd relaxed me to a place beyond words, or if the curse was keeping me quiet. I suspected it was a bit of both.

Oblivious to my issues, Tessa completed her inspection of my arms, and moved on to my shoulders. She knelt behind me and paused.

"Eli, what's this in your back?" she murmured, stroking her hand down the length of my spine. Her hand moved lower, toward the darkness within me. The grayish tendrils of the curse snapped a warning, then she paused. "Dan, help me lay her flat."

"Why isn't she responsive?"

"She's too deep in her trance." The cushion was moved aside, then I felt Tessa's hands under my armpits and Dan's under my thighs as they laid me flat on my back. "But she can hear us, and knows exactly what we're doing."

"I think I messed up the circle," Dan said.

Tessa didn't answer him. Instead, she pressed her hands over my heart, then my stomach. She followed the tendrils down to my lower abdomen, then she gasped.

"What is it?" Dan demanded. "Is she okay?"

"The curse is in her womb."

I was still out of it as Tessa blew out the candles, and Dan bundled me into a blanket and carried me inside the house. After he situated me on the couch, I heard him and Tessa talking in the kitchen.

"How long will she be asleep?" he asked.

"She's not sleeping, she's entranced," Tessa said. "As for how long she'll remain entranced, it's hard to say. Alex sometimes goes in so deep it takes him days to surface, and Eli does take after him."

"Speaking of taking after, did this curse offer any clues as to who put it on Eli in the first place?"

"No, but there is a decidedly feminine feel to it."

"Great. We only have half the population to work through." I heard the fridge door open and shut. "Think it was her mother?"

"I don't know. Honestly, I know very little about Christina, so I can't speak to her motivations, but she was Eli's mother. Why would a mother curse her child? And her womb, no less."

Dan grunted, which was his go-to response when felt he was in over his head. "Should we take her to a doctor?"

"I don't need a doctor," I mumbled.

"You mean a conventional mortal doctor?" Tessa asked. Evidently, they hadn't heard me. "And tell the doctor what, that she's about to birth a curse?"

"Is that going to happen?" Dan asked. "Will it... come out of her?"

"No doctor," I said, a little louder. When they kept talking, I waved my arm to get their attention, and rolled right off the couch.

"Hey, babe," Dan said as he lifted me off the floor. "You going somewhere?"

"No doctor," I mumbled. Dan sat on the couch with me on his lap. "Hate them."

"All right. No doctors."

Tessa smoothed back my hair. "Eli, honey, you'll be out of it for a while yet. Want me to wait and drive you home?"

I pried my eyelids open and stared at Dan. "Can I stay here?"

"Of course you can."

Tessa squeezed my shoulder. "Call me when you're up to it," she said, and she let herself out of Dan's house. Once she was gone, Dan tightened his arms around me.

"Tell me what you need," he murmured against my forehead.

"I'm fine," I said. "Tessa's right. It takes a bit to come back from a trance."

"I don't like seeing you like that. Scary."

"After everything that happened the other day—witches, car crashes, and the rest—me lying on the ground is scary?"

"Yeah, well."

Dan didn't say anything further, but as he tucked my head underneath his chin, I realized why he was so nervous. His wife had died right here in this house, and I bet he was the one who found her.

"I'm sorry," I said. "I should have prepared you for what it would look like."

"It's okay. I know for next time." He paused before asking, "Does it hurt? The curse, I mean."

"I didn't even know it was there." I swallowed. "What do you think it means?"

"Hell if I know, but we'll figure it out. We always do."

Thornapple is available wherever books are sold. Find a print or electronic version here: https://books2read.com/poisongarden-thornapple

About the Author

Jennifer Allis Provost is a native New Englander who lives in a sprawling colonial along with her beautiful and precocious twins, a dog that thinks she's a kangaroo, a parrot, a junkyard cat, and a wonderful husband who never forgets to buy ice cream. As a child, she read anything and everything she could get her hands on, including a set of encyclopedias, but fantasy was always her favorite. She spends her days drinking vast amounts of coffee, arguing with her computer, and avoiding any and all domestic behavior.

Find Jenn on the web here: http://authorjenniferallisprovost.com/

For up to the minute sale notifications, follow her on Bookbub here: https://www.bookbub.com/profile/jennifer-allis-provost

For exclusive content, follow her on Patreon: https://www.patreon.com/jenniferallisprovost/

Friend her on Facebook: http://www.facebook.com/jennallis

Follow her on Instagram: @jenniferaprovost

Happy reading!

ALSO BY JENNIFER ALLIS PROVOST

The Chronicles of Parthalan, a six volume epic fantasy (and one short story collection)

Heir to the Sun

The Virgin Queen

Rise of the Deva'shi

Pieces of Parthalan: All-New Stories From The Land Of Parthalan

Golem

Elfsong

Sunfall

The Copper Legacy, a four book urban fantasy:

Copper Girl

Copper Ravens

Copper Veins

Copper Princess

A duology based in the Copper world:

Redemption

Salvation

Poison Garden, an urban fantasy filled with seers, witches, and one seriously hot detective:

Belladonna

Oleander

Bleeding Hearts

Thornapple

Gallowglass, an urban fantasy set in Scotland and New York:

Gallowglass

Walker

Homecoming

Winter's Queen, an urban fantasy set in Scotland and Elphame:

Touch of Frost

Giant's Daughter

Elphame's Queen

Changes, a contemporary romance:

Changing Teams

Changing Scenes

Changing Fate

Changing Dates